SHE FROM THE GUTTA 2

BRIANN DANAE

Copyrighted Material

Copyright © 2018 BriAnn Danae
Cover art by **Beyond the Book Cover Designs**
Published by **Beyond the Book Publications**

All rights reserved. No part of this book may be reproduced in any form without written consent of the publisher, except brief quotations in review form.

This is a work of fiction. Any characters, places, objects, references or similarities to actual events, real people, living or dead, or to real locals are intended to give the novel a sense of reality. Any similarity in other names, characters, places, and incidents are entirely coincidental and are solely of the Author's imagination.

Written by
BriAnn Danae

CHAPTER ONE

A million and one thoughts ran through Enzo's mind as his bulged eyes darted between Zeema and Harlem. The thought that was at the forefront of his brain was why the hell Harlem had jumped in front of this snake ass female. Seeing the pained expression on Harlem's face, and blood seeping through her shirt had Enzo taking a quick step in her direction.

"Oh my gosh. Y-You shot me," Harlem choked out in pain.

Pulling her hand away from her shoulder where the bullet had entered, her eyes watered when she saw blood decorating her palm. Enzo stared down at her angrily.

"What the fuck you jump in front of her for!?" he all but hollered, as his jaw clenched.

Slapping her hand away, he assessed her wound and let

out a sigh of relief when he saw it was a clean shot. The bullet had gone straight through her shoulder, out her back and into the wall. Though a clean shot, Enzo was still pissed off.

"Oh my gosh!" Zeema squealed, hugging Harlem from the back. "Thank you so much."

Shaking her off, Harlem smacked her hand away and looked down at the hand Enzo held out for her to take. He didn't want to help her ass up. When Harlem stood to her feet, unwilling to take his hand, and brushed past him, he sucked his teeth.

With his attention focused on where the bullet had gone, Enzo was halfway grateful it hadn't landed somewhere in Harlem's body that would've killed her. He was only halfway grateful because he wished its final destination was burning hot inside Zeema's head. Enzo mugged her as she swiped tears from her cheeks. When her vision cleared, she stared over at Trill's lifeless body before her eyes quickly darted up at Enzo.

"Don't do it," Harlem let out.

Enzo's trigger finger was itching to end her life. The bitch had no business being there in the first place and now Harlem wanted to save her... and for what?

"What? You leaving witnesses now cause she's carrying a baby she's probably lying about?" he spat Harlem's way.

"I'm not lying!" Zeema squealed, placing a hand over her stomach.

Harlem grilled her with evil eyes. "Shut the fuck up."

"You need to figure something out and hurry your ass up," Enzo huffed annoyed as hell.

Enzo nor Harlem thought they'd have to end Trill's life tonight, but Enzo was prepared for whatever. He had a crew of two men who were waiting for him near the gate to handle Trill's body and the cleaning up afterwards. Quickly, Harlem thought about what she was about to do with Zeema. Clearly, the bitch couldn't hold water so there was no way she was about to just let her walk out of the house scot-free. No, there was no way. Plus, Harlem wanted, no needed, answers.

The only thing she could think of at the time was to hold her hostage. As heartless as Harlem was, she couldn't see herself killing a pregnant woman, if Zeema was in fact with child. The blood on her hands from killing Trill was already eating her alive. *I'm not a killer*, she thought to herself.

"Give me your keys," she demanded with an outstretched hand Zeema's way. Zeema had a dumbfounded look on her face and Enzo shook his head.

As bad as he wanted to bombard Harlem with questions about this so-called pregnancy Zeema had run her big ass mouth about, he knew they needed to get the fuck up out of Trill's crib first and get her medical treatment. The fact that he was contemplating on having such a conversation was baffling to him. Harlem of all people had really pulled a fast one on him, but he was hoping like hell Zeema was lying. Something deep down inside told him she wasn't though.

"M-My keys? For what?" Zeema stuttered.

"Give me your keys or lose your life," Harlem stated calmly.

With trembling limbs, Zeema opened her closed fist where her keys had been in and handed them over to Harlem. Being two steps ahead of her, Enzo snatched them from her and stuffed them in his pocket.

"If you think you about to drive her car somewhere with her in it, you got me fucked up," he told her.

"What? You don't trust me now?"

"Should I?" Enzo shot back, as they stared one another down.

Harlem's nose flared, and teeth gritted at his question. She knew what he was hinting at, but he had no fucking right to. She wasn't the one who up and left him. Rolling her eyes, Harlem took one last glance at Trill and her eyes softened. She really hated she had to be the one to take him out, but that was how the game went. Kill or be killed.

"Go get that nigga's phone," Enzo told her before she reached the front door.

Turning on her heels, she shot him a mean mug but made her way up the steps like she was told. Inside the bedroom, Harlem saw his phone lighting up with an incoming call. Snatching it and the charger up, Harlem powered the phone off. She knew that was his main phone, so quickly, she scanned the room for his Android he used for business purposes. When she spotted it on the opposite side of the bed, she walked around the bed and pocketed it before heading back downstairs.

Walking out with a gun to Zeema's back, a firm grip on her arm and one duffel bag of money hanging from each shoulder, Enzo scowled at Harlem. He couldn't believe her. Opening the back door on the driver's side, Enzo tossed Zeema in and climbed in after her.

"You drive since you wanted to keep this bitch alive."

"My shoulder," Harlem growled.

Enzo gave her a blank stare. "Didn't nobody tell your ass to jump in front of her. I'll call somebody to come look at it. And, I hope you dropping her off somewhere, because we need to talk," he hissed.

"I'm not in the mood right now."

"You heard what I said," he said and closed the door.

Releasing a deep sigh, Harlem carefully climbed into the driver's seat of the car and adjusted it, so she could reach the steering wheel. Thankfully, she had been shot in her right shoulder, so she could still drive with her left hand. Enzo semi cared about the pain she was in, but he wanted to teach her ass a lesson. As she slowly pulled out of the driveway, a nauseous feeling came over her. She was overwhelmed with everything that had just gone down, but she knew this wasn't the end of it all. It never was.

"Pull up on the side of this van," Enzo instructed.

When she did, Enzo let his window down and tossed the

driver Zeema's keys. The driver handed Enzo a cd, and no words were exchanged as he let the window back up. The men in the van already knew he'd text them instructions about her car once they handled Trill. Harlem's breathing was ragged and as hard as she tried to calm her rapidly beating heart down, she couldn't. Every few seconds, her eyes would scan her side mirrors before peeping into the rearview. At the time of morning it was, there were only a few cars out heading to work, but Harlem could never be too sure about someone following them. Her paranoia was at an all-time high.

"You good?" Enzo asked her, and she nodded.

"Where are we going?" Zeema questioned.

Harlem nor Enzo answered her. Instead, Harlem picked her phone up out of the cup holder and unlocked it. Going to Dreka's name in her call log, she tapped her name and the phone rang loudly in her ear. She turned the volume down some as soon as Dreka answered in her groggy tone.

"Yeah?"

"I need a favor," Harlem let out, clearing her throat.

Hearing the urgency in Harlem's voice, Dreka sat up in her bed and wiped the sleep from her eyes. She knew whatever her friend was calling her at this hour for had to be of some importance.

"What you need me to do?"

Dreka was trained to go. Whether Harlem gave her all the details right now or not, she was ready for whatever.

That's how the two had been since day one and nothing was going to change.

"Ask your brother if he can keep an eye on something for me."

"What! I don't need anyone to—"

The grip Enzo had on her arm got tighter. Shooting him a menacing look, Enzo stared back at her evilly. He didn't give a fuck what Harlem had up her sleeve, but what he didn't need Zeema doing was speaking. Her entire existence was pissing him off. Snatching his mask up, Enzo forced it over her head, so the front part was facing the back. She was already talking too much, and her sight most definitely wasn't needed.

"Get yo' ass on the floor and be quiet," Enzo grumbled. When she didn't move, Enzo tapped her head with the barrel of his gun and she immediately dropped to the ground. "Shoulda just offed this broad, man."

Harlem looked at him through the rearview, but Enzo didn't make eye contact with her. He was pissed off and even the money they had come up on wasn't lightening his mood. On the other end of the phone, Dreka had clicked over and called her brother. Vonzell wasn't wrapped too tight. In fact, he wasn't sane at all. Having seen and been through way too much at a young age, Vonzell had a thing for seeing people suffer. It was a sick fetish of his, but it only came out when need be, and Harlem needed his services.

Clicking back over, Dreka rolled her eyes before saying,

"He said yeah. Meet him at the spot. Want me to meet you there?"

"Nah. I'll get you hip later. Thank you."

"You know it's nothing. Be safe."

Harlem told her she would and hung up. With all the licks she and Dreka had hit together, Zeema hadn't been let in on every little aspect of their operation, which came in handy today. Enzo didn't know who the hell she had just spoken with or where they were going, but he was ready to lay low. His phone was blowing up with calls from Lucci and Briscoe, but there was no way he was about to answer them.

When Harlem pulled up to a deserted location with houses that were barely standing, Enzo just knew she was on some bullshit.

"You seriously about to drop this broad off? You trust whoever you were talking to like that?" he asked.

Harlem nodded. "I do. I don't have time to watch her all day."

"The fuck you let her live for then?"

"Because it's not up to me who gets to live and who gets to die. Or did you forget that I'm not God?" she spat back.

A silence fell over the car. She had a point, but Enzo didn't care. Zeema was a liability and the more people Harlem tried bringing in on whatever scheme she had quickly devised, Enzo wasn't feeling. But, this was her idea and at this point, he just wanted to get home. Letting out a deep sigh, Harlem got out of the car and walked around to the side

Zeema was on. Snatching her out once the door was open, she shoved her toward the old wooden steps, and onto the porch. Vonzell opened the door and let them in. Enzo hopped out, climbing into the driver's seat. He didn't want to meet whoever Harlem was involved with. She clearly had a poor sense of judgement.

The darkness had Zeema shivering. Never did she think her grimy ways would catch up to her, especially not this soon. Once again, she had been caught slipping and Enzo had spared her life. It had happened twice already, and she'd bet her last, if given the opportunity, he wouldn't give her a third chance to live. Shoving her ahead, Harlem rolled her eyes.

Though she wanted to get to the bottom of why Zeema had coincidentally popped up at Trill's crib, she knew now wasn't the time nor the place. Vonzell's grayish-green eyes were staring coldly at her like she was the one he had to keep an eye on. Had he not been batshit crazy, Harlem would consider him to be a little cute. His crazy ways made her see him in a different light though.

"You were awake?" she asked, and he nodded.

"I'm always up. How long you need me to watch her?"

Harlem nibbled on her bottom lip. "Umm, I'll get with you on that. I know for a few days for sure. I'll text you before I come by."

Vonzell nodded. "Aight. Anything off limits?"

His tone dropped an octave lower, letting Harlem know he was ready to cause true damage if given the green light.

She could have easily just told him not to kill her, but Vonzell needed clear, detailed instructions.

"No rape or hitting her. If she gets out of line, it's up to you. But, no hitting unless provoked. Oh, and she claims she's pregnant, so you can feed the bitch if you want to. That's up to you though."

A satisfied smirk covered his face as he grabbed Zeema's arm. A silver chair sat in the middle of the shabby, scuffed hardwood floors with duct tape, thick poly-manila rope, a blowtorch, and a pair of dice next to it. Harlem had no clue what the dice were for, and she didn't even want to guess knowing Vonzell. Tossing Zeema into the chair with force, Vonzell pulled a pair of handcuffs out of his back pocket. Grabbing her wrists, Zeema shouted muffled obscenities behind the mask as he cuffed her wrists behind her back. He'd save tying her ankles up once he fucked with her for a little bit.

Walking over to her, Harlem snatched the mask from off her head. Zeema gasped for air as she looked up into Harlem's eyes. Gone were her tears; she was angry but could only blame herself.

"Harlem I-" she began, but Harlem cut her off by lifting her hand.

"I'm not trying to hear all of that bullshit right now. When I come back, you better be ready to talk. As much grimy shit you done pulled in the last few months, I can't even imagine what you were doing there tonight. Maybe sitting here for a while will give you time to think, and hopefully it's about the truth," Harlem told her.

When she went to speak again, a piece of duct tape was placed roughly over her mouth. Vonzell could tell just from the words she barely got out that she was going to be fun to torture. Hearing her talk right now wasn't in the plans though. Harlem shook her head as Zeema tried pleading with her eyes. Had Zeema not crossed her once before, she might have given her a chance to speak, but Harlem knew better. Or, she was learning to anyway. Once a snake bites you, it doesn't change its colors; it just sheds its skin. It was still a snake regardless of the new body it was in and Zeema was living proof.

"I'll bring your money when I come back," she told Vonzell once she made it to the door.

"Aight. I know you're good for it."

"I appreciate you. Don't get too crazy. I want her alive the next time I see her," she scolded him with a stern look.

Vonzell gave her a tightlipped grin and opened the door. "I heard you the first time. Get out."

Anyone else would have been stunned by his rudeness or even ready to pop off, but Harlem was used to it and she knew it was just how Vonzell was. Climbing into the passenger seat, she slammed the door and Enzo looked over at her.

"Done being captain save a hoe?" he asked sarcastically.

Releasing a deep breath, Harlem ignored him.

Amused by her behavior, Enzo let out a chuckle. "You can't talk now?"

"Stop talking to me and just take me home."

"Why? So, you can cry over that dead ass nigga in peace?"

Harlem looked over at him as he pulled off down the street and sucked her teeth. Enzo could most definitely be an asshole when he wanted to be, but she wasn't in the mood for his shit. Too much had gone down tonight for him to be testing her. After a few minutes of silence, Enzo spoke up. His raspy voice invaded the tight space that seemed to be suffocating them both.

"You don't have anything to tell me?" he asked.

"Nope."

Her one-word reply made Enzo's body turn hot. He knew she was lying, but there was no need to anymore. The subject of her supposedly being pregnant wasn't one he was backing down from; he didn't give a fuck what she didn't feel like discussing. She had better start feeling like it because he needed answers.

"So, you a liar now? Good girl Harlem with all these fucking secrets, huh? What happened to the girl I used to know?"

An ache simultaneously traveled through her chest and throat. Staring at the side of his head, Harlem had the right mind to mush him in it, but putting her hands on a man wasn't her thing. That violent shit was never her thing and it wouldn't be now. No matter how mad Enzo had her in the moment she'd never lay a hand on him because she damn sure didn't want him to lay one on her. Enzo never would though, so she had nothing to worry about.

Enzo glanced her way before focusing back on the road. "What you sitting there looking crazy for? Talk."

"Fuck you, Enzo," she hissed.

"Fuck me? Fuck me for what? I haven't done a damn thing to you."

"You left me!" Harlem screamed, feeling the tears gather in her tired eyes.

Slamming her back into the seat, her right leg bounced uncontrollably as she stared out of the window. Being in the car with him right now was too much. Him asking her questions about some shit she knew he wasn't ready for was too painful. The past was called the past for a reason. It was something Harlem never brought up. The people close to her didn't either and knew not to. Well, everyone except Zeema.

She sniffled and shook her head. "You left me and expected for everything to be the same when you returned. That was selfish. You're selfish for even thinking it could be."

"Place all the blame on me; I'll take that. If me leaving so neither one of us ended up in jail makes me the bad guy, cool. I'll do it all over again. But, let's not forget why we're having this conversation in the first place. You're avoiding my main question. You were pregnant?"

Licking her lips, Harlem sniffled again and sighed. "It

doesn't matter if I was or not. You weren't here, and it probably wasn't yours anyway."

The car swerved some as Enzo damn near broke his neck to look her way. Harlem stared straight ahead, unbothered by his menacing eyes burning a hole into the side of her face.

Enzo had to chuckle to keep from tossing her ass the fuck out of the car in the middle of the road. "Probably wasn't mine," he scoffed and shook his head. "So not only are you a liar but a hoe too? Damn. I really did fuck you up."

"Yo mama's a hoe, nigga. Don't fucking play with me."

Enzo wanted to laugh, but he didn't play about his mama. "My mama ain't got shit to do with you busting that little pussy open for the next nigga. What? You let some nigga run up in you raw and knock you up right when I left? You didn't love a nigga for real if that's the type of shit you were on," he grumbled lowly, not believing this was the direction their conversation had taken.

Had this been any other time, Harlem would have laughed. Enzo was pissed. Of course, she hadn't let some nigga run up in her raw, or at all. Not until she was with Kartel, but that was months later.

"Can't really fuck another nigga with a broken heart. I had nothing to give to the next man because you took it and ran off to who knows where. So, you don't get to question me about anything. Not shit! Especially not tonight. After what just went down, I need some time away from you and this lifestyle. It's too much."

"You really caught feelings for this nigga, huh?" Enzo asked incredulously, sounding pissed off and even a little hurt.

Harlem's silent reply was all the confirmation he needed. He couldn't believe she had fallen for a lick. *What the hell did that nigga do to her?* Enzo questioned to himself.

"Well, he's dead now so oh well. Bury them feelings right along with his body when that time comes," he said evenly, with no remorse.

"You're an asshole," Harlem spat.

"Takes one to know one, baby. You should be used to me by now. You better hope that scandalous bitch doesn't snitch on us. You and I both know the only female popping up at a nigga crib like that, is one he's fucking. And, she pregnant?" he scoffed. "She's a liability for real. Been a headache since day one and you decided to befriend her."

As Enzo shook his head, Harlem was thinking the same thing. Really, all the signs had been there as far as Zeema not being a trustworthy friend, but Harlem overlooked them. The money they were getting together had mentally blinded her judgement. Females like Zeema always had ulterior motives. It may not have been immediately, but she knew one day they would surface.

"Okay. It's too late now, so just drop it. She's not going to snitch."

"Yeah, aight," was Enzo's only reply.

Instead of going to his crib like he first planned to do back at Vonzell's hideaway, Enzo headed to Harlem's crib. He was going to take her home, but he wasn't letting her out of the car until she answered at least one of his questions. Whether that be truthfully or not, he just needed some type of reassurance. When he pulled onto her block, it was still dark out, but the birds were chirping loudly in the nearby trees.

Pulling into the driveway, he placed the car in park. Enzo locked the doors and pressed a button to lock them permanently until he decided to let her out. Huffing, Harlem looked over at him. As upset and hurt as she was, she couldn't deny how sexy Enzo looked busting his gun. Seeing him in action, protecting them back at Trill's house, had nasty thoughts floating through her mind, but not anymore. She just wanted to get out of his presence for a few days and clear her head.

"You have me locked in here for a reason. What more could you possibly want from me right now?" she questioned.

Enzo was glad she asked. "The truth. I mean, if you can remember what that is."

Harlem's jaw clenched. His smart mouth was really pissing her off. Closing her eyes, she took a deep breath and released it slowly. "The truth about what? Be specific because I'm only good for one question with one answer right now and that's it until I decide to divulge more."

"Were you pregnant and was it mine?"

Harlem cocked her head to the side. "That was two questions."

"One sentence, though. So, it counts."

She knew there was going to be no winning with him. Plus, he hadn't asked the one question she was dreading to hear spill from his lips, so that was a good thing. These questions she could answer and truthfully at that.

"Yes, to both."

The grip he had on the steering wheel tightened as his head dropped and shoulders slouched defeatedly. Enzo couldn't even look at Harlem anymore. Not right now at least. The same way she needed a few days away from him, is the same way he was feeling about her. Pressing the button to unlock the locks, he unlocked the doors for her. Harlem's voice got caught in her throat when she tried to speak. Clearing it, she licked her lips before speaking.

"That's it? What about counting the money up?"

Enzo lifted his head and gave her a look she had never seen before. One that had her damn near ready to run from the car.

"The money? Is that all you care about?" he spat through clenched teeth.

"What else is there to care about? There ain't no love in this shit, remember? Didn't you teach me that?" she replied smoothly.

Enzo couldn't believe her. Harlem was shocking the hell out of him, but he shouldn't have been surprised. Had she not changed with the lifestyle she was living, he'd for sure think something was off with her.

"Nah," he chuckled in disbelief. "I told you there was no

love for any other nigga in this shit except for me, but I guess I'm not exempt, huh?"

Harlem shrugged. "I guess not. Don't take it personal. I'm sure you understand."

Not offering up another word, afraid that she might break down in tears, Harlem grabbed the duffle bag she had placed on the passenger side floor with her good arm and climbed out. Rushing inside her home, she dropped the bag from her shoulder, locked the door, and slid down it. Her chest tightened immediately as she was on the verge of a mini panic attack. With her eyes closed, she slowly coached herself through it after five minutes. When her phone vibrated, Harlem peeled her eyes open and grabbed it from the pocket of her hoodie. A text from Enzo is what graced her eyes. She didn't even have to open it to read it.

I got somebody five minutes out to come clean your wound.

Instead of replying, she just liked his text. Harlem was thankful he still cared enough to make sure her wound was good. It hurt like hell, but it certainly could've been worse. When her phone vibrated again, she sighed knowing it was Enzo.

Damn you don't love me no more

There was no question mark at the end, so Harlem could only assume that he was making a statement rather than asking a question. Their normal parting words went unsaid tonight, and Enzo immediately felt the shift in their relationship already. She didn't even bother to reply as one lone tear slid down her cheek. She wasn't crying because of his question, but more so the reality of her life once again. Her love for Enzo or her love for the lifestyle she was living was the cause of Trill's death. That right there was the scary part of it all. Either way it went, love had gotten someone killed yet again and their blood was on her hands.

This had been the latest Harlem had slept in in months. Her body would normally wake up on its own every morning around five-forty-five, and she'd be ready to start her day. Not today though. The pain pills Cole, the female street doctor Lucci had on payroll, gave her last night had her sleeping like a baby. Harlem only saved a few and flushed the rest down the toilet, though. Seeing what they had done to her mama had her cautious of becoming addicted.

Sitting up, she yawned and shook her head when she heard her alarm system going off. She knew it could only be one of two people popping up on her, and she'd bet her last it was Yazmin.

"Harlem!" Yaz yelled out as she crossed the threshold of her friend's front door.

Not bothering to reply, Harlem simply grabbed her phone from her dresser and looked at the time and hundreds of notifications. A few were from Enzo, and she tapped the 'x' in the corner to erase them. The missed calls were from unknown numbers and a few from Yaz.

"It's too early for this bullshit," she grumbled, adjusting in her bed. Wincing, she touched her patched up shoulder. She couldn't believe Enzo had really shot her. Though not purposely, Harlem was still in shock.

"I'm glad you're alive," Yaz said as she walked inside her bedroom.

"Thanks," Harlem replied dryly.

Yaz shot her a stank look, but her eyes perked up when she saw Harlem's shoulder bandaged up. "What the hell happened to you?"

"Enzo shot me."

"He what!"

Yaz yelled so loud, Harlem squeezed her eyes tight, hating the pain she felt coming on in the form of a headache. She knew Yaz was dramatic, but this was one of those days where she needed her to relax just a tad.

"I know you didn't just sit here with a straight face and tell me he shot you?" Yaz pressed.

"I did. I mean, it was kind of my fault, but still."

"Your fault! How is someone else shooting you your fault? What, you jumped in front of his gun or something?"

It was uncanny the way Yaz assumed things and was spot on. When Harlem didn't answer her right away, Yaz shook her head and took a seat at the end of the bed facing her.

"Y'all are fucking crazy. The nigga was blowing my

phone up all morning, while I was in bed with my man, telling me to come check on you only to find out he's the reason you're laid up in pain. What the hell happened?"

Harlem battled with herself about giving Yaz the full story of what all went down. She knew she could trust her with her life, that she knew, but she wasn't sure about including Trill's death. Though she'd never admit it to anyone, not yet at least, Harlem was really in her feelings about killing him.

"A lot. Some shit that shouldn't have even gone down, honestly," she said, shaking her head sadly. "Let me brush my teeth and pee and I'll tell you what happened."

"Okay. You need help or you good?"

Harlem was in pain, but she was good. "I'm fine."

Yaz played around on her phone and sent Enzo a mad face once she thought about him shooting her girl. Enzo didn't even reply, he knew exactly why she had sent him that damn emoji. The only person she needed to be mad at was Harlem, though. When Harlem was done handling her hygiene, she climbed back into the bed and sighed before she started to fill Yaz in on the events of last night.

The facial expressions Yaz wore while Harlem spoke were a mixture of shock, sadness, anger, and confusion. They were all the emotions Harlem had felt as well, but on a grander scale. When she was finished, she took a deep breath waiting for Yaz to say something.

"I-I'm seriously at a loss for words and that never happens," Yaz let out.

"You and me both."

"So, this bitch Zeema... what we gone do about her? I swear you should have let Enzo kill her. You already know how I feel about her, but what I can't understand is why you jumping in front of bitches who probably wouldn't do the same in return? And, she snitching? The fuck is up with you?"

Yaz was perplexed. She couldn't understand for the life of her why Harlem decided to save a bitch who was nothing but trouble and had been from the jump.

"She's pregnant, Yaz," Harlem said and Yaz' entire face balled up into a scowl.

"Okay? What is that supposed to mean? She was in the wrong place at the wrong fucking time. Oh well! The bitch probably lied and look at you, ready to play hero. You ain't gone learn until she really does something grimy to your ass."

Harlem was getting upset. "Her unborn has nothing to do with the beef between us. I couldn't just let him kill her."

"Why? And please don't say because of the child y'all created. No. Don't look like that. You know I'm not trying to throw that in your face but come on Harlem. Even I know how this street shit works. No witnesses, yet you saved one, because of what?"

Honestly, Harlem didn't have an answer. At the time, her mind was on how she wasn't necessarily given the chance to be a mother to the child she and Enzo created. Another part of her felt guilty because Zeema, along with Yaz and Sarena, had helped her heal once she slipped into depression back then. Killing her was the code she knew the streets went by, but she just couldn't.

"I just couldn't, okay? I'm not a murderer," she cried, shaking her head.

Standing up, Yaz stepped over to her and rubbed her back. "I mean, you kind of are, but I understand. I'm trying to at least. She had no right to air your business out like that, but I definitely see where Enzo is coming from. You can't trust Zeema. You may have wanted to leave her alive because you felt guilty, but you gone really feel like shit if she snitches."

Harlem heard her loud and clear, but she knew there was no way Zeema could snitch even if she wanted to. Vonzell wouldn't hesitate to place a bullet in her head the minute she forced his hand. Zeema wasn't her main concern right now. Enzo was. She knew for a fact the brief conversation they had last night wasn't over. Enzo was relentless when it came to something he wanted. He wanted the truth and wouldn't stop until Harlem fessed up.

"The nigga didn't even apologize for shooting me," Harlem hissed as Yaz sat back on the bed.

Laughing, Yaz shook her head. "Bitch, you practically shot yourself. I ain't apologizing either if I was him."

Harlem snickered. Of course, she'd say some bullshit like

that. They sat in silence and deep thought for a few seconds until Yaz spoke up.

"So, what's your next move? You can't hide out in this house for the rest of your life."

"I'm going to wait until the shit with Trill dies down a bit."

"You gon' go to his funeral?"

Harlem hadn't even thought of that. "Nah. No one knew I was fucking with him. No need for the unwanted attention."

Yaz just nodded. Even if she wanted to go to the funeral, it'd be no point. There'd be no body to view or lay to rest. Enzo made sure of that. What Harlem did know was that after last night's chaos, she needed to sit down and chill her ass out. Things could have gone much worse than they had, and she could only imagine how things would have gone had the bullet caused life threatening injuries.

Just as she picked her phone up, a text from Vonzell came through. Opening it, Harlem smirked at the picture he sent her of Zeema, bloodied and bruised up. Erasing it, she made a mental reminder to stop by in a few days and check-in with them. Letting her sit in agony and pain to suffer was much better than killing her right away. A slow and gruesome death, if it came to that, is what a bitch like Zeema deserved. It was only right.

CHAPTER TWO

"You really in love, huh?"

Enzo looked over at Lucci, who wore a smirk on his face and shrugged his shoulders. If that's what his cousin wanted to call it, then that's what it was.

"What made you say that?" Enzo asked.

"From the shit you just told me, only a nigga who's in love with a broad would've let that shit go down. It's cool if you are," Lucci snickered.

Enzo couldn't help but grin and just wave him off. He wasn't in love with Harlem. Hell, he didn't even know what it meant to be *in love*, but he loved her no doubt. His love ran so deep for her; he had to literally force himself to stay busy, so he wouldn't pop up over her crib.

"I really didn't have a choice, to be honest," Enzo replied.

"On the real? You shoulda just offed the bitch and dealt

with the consequences later. What was Harlem gon' do? Bring her back from the dead?"

Lucci had the nerve to chuckle, but he had a point. Harlem would've had to just be mad if he was in Enzo's shoes. Wasn't no bitch, especially Zeema, about to hold a murder over his head.

"I was going to until she jumped her silly ass in front of her. I'm still hot about that shit."

"As you should be. So, what's next? Dreka brother somebody you trust?"

Enzo shrugged. "I don't know that nigga, but Harlem clearly trusts him. Forget all that though. What the streets talkin' about?"

Once news got out about the murders of Trill and six of his crew members, the town was in disbelief. Speculations were going around that they had been set up by someone on the inside, and that was cool with Enzo. The less heat that was brought his and his niggas' way, the better. The last thing he wanted to be dealing with was a murder charge. Thanks to his cleanup men, all traces of he and Harlem ever stepping foot in Trill's house that night were erased.

"You know they in shambles but fuck it. Them niggas had it coming."

Nodding, Enzo agreed. "Yeah. I just can't believe she caught feelings for that nigga, man. That's wild."

"Yo! Wild as fuck. I ain't think sis was going out bad like that. But can you blame her?"

Enzo's face immediately frowned up. "Can I blame her? What's that supposed to mean?"

"Aww, here you go about to get in your feelings. You left her, remember? If she was married with kids when you popped your ass back up, the fuck would you be mad for?"

"The fuck you think, nigga?"

Enzo was getting pissed off. The last person to try and preach to him about his situation was Lucci. He had fucked best friends, cousins, sisters, shit aunties and all, but wanted to try and spit some knowledge to his cousin. Enzo wasn't nearly in the mood, but he was going to listen just to see what Lucci had to say.

Lucci stared him in the eyes and asked, "She was supposed to wait for you?"

"Yeah."

Laughing, Lucci shook his head. For once in his life, he couldn't agree with his cousin. Had he not spent five years in jail thinking the same thing about a few females he thought was down for him, he'd probably be on Enzo's side, but not today.

"Nah. Had you not left her the way you did, she probably would have. You was down in the 'D' with a whole bitch."

Enzo sucked his teeth. "Man, you know that shit with Arie wasn't nothing but me getting my dick wet."

"I ain't talkin' about Arie, nigga," Lucci said, giving him a pensive glare just as the doorbell rang.

Saved by the bell, Enzo thought as Lucci stood to answer

the door. Did he have a right to be upset for Harlem not waiting around for him? Sure. Was it going to change how she felt about him leaving? Absolutely not, and Enzo needed to understand that life went on without him. Whether he wanted it to or not wasn't his choice.

"Just the nigga I was looking for," Yaz said as she strutted through Lucci's living room as if she owned it.

She had just gotten off work and decided to pop up over Lucci's crib, and she was glad she had. Mushing Enzo upside his head, she mugged him while taking a seat on the couch across from him.

"You got my friend fucked up," she hissed.

"Don't come in here on that bullshit, Yazmin," Lucci fussed, flopping down next to her.

"I'm just saying. You sitting up over here like you didn't shoot my girl."

Enzo smirked. "I ain't mean to."

"Yeah? Your ass must have forgotten how to apologize too. Sloppy ass nigga," she hissed and Lucci slapped her thigh.

"Chill out. What they got going on ain't none of your business."

"It's not yours either, but I bet that's what y'all were over here gossiping about," she eyed them both with her lips tooted out. When they didn't reply, she continued. "Exactly."

Enzo stood to his feet. "I ain't ever gossiped in my life with yo big head ass."

"Fuck you. You need to go check on my friend. Matter of fact... don't. Let one of her other niggas cater to her."

Yaz smirked when she saw Enzo's jaw tighten. That's all it took for him to get riled up and she knew it. He hated that he showed his hand every time when it came to Harlem, but he couldn't help it. She had his mind gone, and with the new information she dropped like a bomb on him a few days ago, Harlem had Enzo by the balls, and she didn't even know it.

"She ain't got no other nigga," Enzo voiced.

"Mhm. Let you tell it."

Lucci stood up and walked behind Enzo as he headed for the door. "Where you about to go?"

"Swing by my mama's crib right quick. See what she and Eli on."

Lucci grinned. "That lil' nigga got big. He damn near taller than me."

"And he don't wanna do nothing with all that height, but it's cool. Sports ain't for everybody."

They slapped hands. "Hell nah, it ain't. Let him do his own thing. Be his own man."

"Most definitely," Enzo nodded. "You and Yaz... what's up with that?"

Lucci smirked and looked over his shoulder to make sure she wasn't eavesdropping. "Nothing right now. We just kicking it and shit."

"Or y'all just fucking?" Enzo questioned, already knowing the answer.

"Both. She cool as fuck but she keep throwing this nigga she supposedly got in my face like I give a fuck."

"Look where she at though," Enzo said, smirking.

"Exactly, my nigga. You know how that go. She gone stay poppin' up over here with her single ass," Lucci laughed and Enzo just shook his head.

"I'll hit you up later on."

"Go check on your girl, nigga. Fore' she really do have another nigga catering to her," Lucci grilled him and Enzo waved him off while hopping in his Maserati.

He wasn't worried about no other nigga. Not anymore at least; Harlem had killed him. Walking back into his living room, Lucci eyed Yaz' thick, chocolate thighs in the mustard colored haltered dress she was wearing. Her body had filled out beyond nicely since her high school days, and Lucci was in love with it.

"What you staring at?" Yaz asked him, just as she placed her cell in her purse.

"Yo thick ass. What you doing poppin' up on me?"

"Oh. I can't pop up now?" she asked, standing up.

Lucci towered over her a good three to four inches, but it wasn't drastic. Staring into his dreamy, dark brown eyes, Yaz had to ask herself what she was *really* doing over there as well. When she looked down and saw the imprint in his shorts, she remembered exactly why. Yaz was really trying to keep it friendly with Lucci, seeing as though she had a man. She wasn't trying hard enough, though.

"If I had a chick up in here, you'd be mad."

She grinned. "Me, mad? Never. You ain't my nigga to be tripping on."

Lucci pulled her to him by her waist. "You saying that shit now."

His hands dropped to her ample ass and jiggled her cheeks. Reaching behind her, Yaz grabbed his wrists.

"Stop."

"I ain't doing nothing your ass don't like."

She gave him a blank stare and Lucci backed them up until he was sitting on the couch. Smirking, he removed his hands from around her and scratched his head.

"What's up, Yazmin? What chu' over here for?" he questioned, and she frowned.

"I was just coming to check on you. Heard you may have a baby on the way."

She smirked and Lucci sucked his teeth. "Fuck nah. I'm not running up in no bitch without a glove, ma. You and I both know that."

"Hmm. So, Zeema's baby ain't yours?"

Lucci cocked his head to the side and twisted his lips as if he were saying 'fuck I look like.' "You ain't hear what I just said? The only thing I fucked on her was her mouth. Dassit."

"I guess. She somebody's baby mama, and you better hope it's not yours."

"Or what? You got a whole nigga at home; fuck outta here," he said, waving her off.

Yaz slapped his hand. "We're not talking about me. This is about you."

"Nah. We don't need to talk about anything on the real. All I'm trying to hear is you moaning my name out while you ride this dick. Fuck all that other shit," he said, now stroking his dick that he pulled out of his boxers and shorts.

Yaz swallowed hard and licked her lips. The sight of Lucci's two-toned, caramel colored pole had her mouth watering. The head was a lighter color than the rest of it and had she been a real scandalous female; she'd suck him off. Giving head to another nigga was out of the question though. As if fucking Lucci was any better.

"I don't know what you stroking your dick for; I just want some head," she sassed, tossing a hand on her hip.

Lucci laughed out loud. "You better take yo ass on home for all that. I ain't yo nigga, remember?"

"Whatever. You gone be blowing my line down if I leave, so save that slick talk for the next bitch."

Stepping over to him, Yaz straddled his lap and reached in her purse for the XL Magnum condom she had. Tearing it open, she looked Lucci in the eyes as she slid it over his hardening dick and played around in the wetness between her legs. The thong she had on was moved to the side for easy access. There was no need to even take it off, knowing she'd only slid through for a quickie.

Thrusting upwards, Lucci held onto her waist and

entered her oasis. "Quit playing with me. Your ass already wet than a mufucka."

Yaz bit her bottom lip and smirked. She was super wet, and all Lucci had did was talk his shit, nothing more. She rode him slowly at first, adjusting to his girth and Lucci smacked her hard on the ass.

"Nah. None of that slow shit. We ain't making love. Fuck me," he groaned as Yaz began to do just that.

When he brought her closer to him by her neck, she went to kiss his lips, and Lucci turned his head. He wasn't down with all that kissing shit. He fucked with Yaz, but she was cheating on her nigga and swapping spit wasn't on the agenda, no matter how good her pussy was.

Moaning softly, Yaz rotated her hips and said, "This is the last time. I promise."

Lucci just smirked. The first time she said it was supposed to be the last time, yet here she was again; taking his dick all in her stomach. He didn't care what she was talking about. As bad as she claimed she wanted to be faithful, she wasn't doing a good job at it. Lucci was cool with that, though. For now. Her pussy was too damn good to just kick to the curb. He could guarantee this wouldn't be her last time taking a ride; promises be damned.

Wiggling in the chair Vonzell still had her tied down to, Zeema groaned. She was so damn uncomfortable she wanted to cry. In fact, she had. They were on day three since her arrival and Vonzell hadn't eased up a bit. The morning after she arrived, he was letting her up to use the restroom and she decided to get a little too happy with her feet and kicked him. That was the wrong move. Vonzell hadn't let her up since, and the busted lip she received was well deserved in his opinion.

"Can you please let me go," Zeema begged quietly.

She was dehydrated and extremely weak, but she wasn't going out quietly. Had she not been pregnant, she'd tell him to just kill her, but she had someone else to live for. Vonzell ignored her like he had been doing for the last two hours. Her crying couldn't move him. The smell of urine and feces didn't bother him. Vonzell seemed to be immune to it.

"Pleeease," Zeema cried out in a hoarse voice. "Help! Someone help me!"

Looking her way, Vonzell smirked. The walls were soundproof. Regardless of how loud she screamed or cried, no one would hear her. Struggling to get free, Zeema rubbed her wrists against the tightrope they were tied with. The friction only caused them to sting more. When she went to yell out again, two quick knocks at the door quieted her immediately.

Standing to his feet, Vonzell gave her a menacing glare and stalked to the door. He was only expecting one guest.

Looking out the peephole, he pulled the door open for Harlem with a smug expression on his face. Harlem cleared her throat and rapidly blinked her eyes at the foul stench that smacked her in the face.

"Get in here," Vonzell hissed, pulling her inside by the arm.

Snapping her head his way, Harlem mugged him and swallowed down the bile that threatened to spew from her lips. The smell inside the home was horrendous. She didn't see how he was even talking at the moment, let alone breathing.

Clearing her throat, she asked, "Is she alive?"

Vonzell smirked and nodded his head toward Zeema. Turning around, Harlem immediately peeped the drained look on her face. She looked a mess. A sickly mess. The spooked look on her face made Harlem smile on the inside, but her face was stiff as stone. Lifting her head, Zeema tried showing a sign of pride. Placing the smell on the back burner, Harlem slowly stepped in her direction and with a quick swing of her arm, knocked the wind that was left out of Zeema. The blow was so vicious; the chair tipped over, causing her face to smack against the wooden floor.

"Uuggh," Zeema cried out, but it fell upon deaf ears.

"Pick this bitch up," Harlem demanded with an icy tone.

Vonzell looked at the back of her head like she was the crazy one but did as she said. Blood leaked from Zeema's mouth as she stared with low eyes at Harlem. She cocked her head to the side, daring her to say something reckless. Acting as if she was going to punch her again, Zeema flinched so hard the chair moved. Vonzell chuckled and Harlem shook her head. The bitch wasn't as tough as she pretended. Harlem didn't intend to make her topple over but knocking her the fuck out sure felt good.

"Can you give us a minute?" she asked him.

"You sure? If you wanted her dead, all you had to—"

Harlem lifted her hand and Vonzell stopped talking. He wasn't scared of her by far, but from the look on her face, he wasn't about to test her gangster. Giving a curt nod, he headed into the kitchen to give them some privacy. Grabbing the fold-up chair he had been sitting in, Harlem sat directly in front of Zeema. Dressed in a pair of black distressed jean shorts, black lace onesie, and Louis Vuitton platform booties on, no one would think she was this ruthless female. Crossing her legs, she placed her hands in her lap and smirked before speaking.

"Hmph. You're still alive."

Zeema's jaw clenched. "W-Why are you doing this?"

"Why were you at Trill's that night?"

She got straight to the point. Tons of reasons crossed her mind over the days as to why she had popped up, but until she heard it from Zeema's mouth first, she wasn't settling on her thoughts. They were driving her crazy. Zeema shook her head not wanting to admit the truth. Squeezing her eyes shut, visions of Trill's dead body clouded her brain.

"I didn't know," she let out.

"You didn't know what?"

"T-That he was a lick. I swear I didn't," she replied, opening her eyes. She stared Harlem in her eyes.

The look in her eyes seemed genuine, but Harlem wasn't falling for it. This was the same bitch who had ran her name through the mud to a broad she didn't even know. The same female who had set her up to rob someone she knew. Nah. There was no trusting her.

"But, you were fucking him, correct?" Harlem asked with ease.

That was the one question that had been on her mind since seeing her that night. Deep down, she knew Enzo's assumptions were correct, but she wanted answers for herself. When Zeema nodded, Harlem struggled to keep a straight face. She wasn't upset. No, she was disgusted. To have been fucking on the same nigga as Zeema was making her skin crawl with disappointment. Shaking her head, she chuckled before asking her next question.

"And, let me guess... that child you're carrying is his?"

When Zeema nodded again, Harlem really wanted to punch her again, but she refrained from doing so. She didn't believe for one second that Zeema had no clue she and Trill had been fucking around, but then again, maybe she was somewhat telling the truth. Harlem had never let her in on Trill being a lick. The only person who knew was Dreka, and she knew for a fact, she hadn't said anything to Zeema.

Perhaps, it was all coincidental, but Harlem wasn't falling for that.

"Harlem," Zeema choked out. "You have to believe me."

"You want me to trust you?" She questioned, pointing at herself. "And why the hell would I do that?"

"You trusted me with your other secret. This was all just bad timing and a misunderstanding."

The mention of her 'other secret' made Harlem's jaw tick. "The secret you quickly ran your mouth about to save your own ass, right?"

Zeema dropped her head. She knew there wasn't going to be any winning with Harlem. At least not today. "He was going to kill me."

"And I should have let him. Silly me. Saved your life, for what? This is the third time you've crossed me, Zeema. Number three. You must know that I'm all out of chances to give, right?"

Sniffling, Zeema lifted her head. "Whatever you're going to do, just do it. You have nothing to lose, right? Coldhearted Harlem. Heartbroken by her first love, so she ruins everyone else's life. Is that why you're so mad at the world? You think you're the only one who had someone you love to abandon you? You're not," she hissed lowly.

Harlem almost got in her feelings by her words, but she shook them off. This wasn't about Enzo or him leaving. This had nothing to do with him, but everything to do with loyalty. Zeema wouldn't know what the hell that meant even if it were spelled out and defined to her. Loyalty, in some cases, could be bought, but for how long and at what price? A true friendship, one where you knew without a doubt that the other person had your front and back was priceless. It was now crystal clear to Harlem that Zeema had never had real friends. If she had, she wouldn't be in the predicament she was in.

"This has nothing to do with him. Nothing. This is about you and your shadiness. I see you sitting here has done nothing, so maybe you need a little more time," Harlem said, standing to her feet.

"Wait!" Zeema called out in a cry like tone. "I-I know I don't deserve anything from you, but can you please let me take a bath and eat? I feel so weak."

"Aye!" Harlem called out for Vonzell, who immediately popped out of the kitchen doorway. "Come here."

"You finished?" Vonzell asked.

"Let her take a bath and feed her."

"She got her lip busted the last time I tried letting her go to the restroom. Fuck her," Vonzell growled, mugging Zeema.

Harlem stared at her until she looked her way. "Next time, I'm giving him permission to kill your ass. Anything else?"

Zeema hurriedly shook her head no. "No, no. Thank you. Wait. There is one more thing. Could you send someone to check on the baby? That's it."

Harlem gave her a pensive stare and sighed. "I'll think about it."

A small smile crossed Zeema's face, but it was wiped off when Vonzell mushed her in the head.

"Don't get all fucking happy. She said she'll think about it," he spat.

Shaking her head, Harlem turned on her heels and headed toward the front door. Vonzell was right behind her. Going into her Louis fanny pack, Harlem pulled out a stack of money and handed to him.

"That's your first cut. Two g's. Let's see if you can keep her alive. I'll be back."

Vonzell's crazy ass grinned. "I like this game more each day."

"Bye crazy. Text me on my burner phone if you need me."

He nodded and closed the door with a few locks following once she stepped out onto the porch. Releasing a hard, heavy breath, she welcomed the semi-fresh air.

"I need a shower now, shit."

Hopping in her car, her music began to play as she backed out of the driveway. She was conflicted on what she wanted to do with Zeema. Killing her would be the easiest thing to do, but it was too soon. Letting her go now when Trill had been buried just a few days before was bad timing. She needed to lay low. They all did.

Facebook was a mess over the weekend with the majority

of Trill and his crews' funerals being held. Harlem forced herself to get off and delete the app altogether after she went to his baby mama's page and saw a picture of his daughter rocking a t-shirt with his face on it. That tore Harlem up inside, and knowing she was the cause of the little girl growing up fatherless had her having nightmares.

For the past week, she'd been waking up in cold sweats. Every dream was of Trill confessing his love for her and it ended with his brains splattering in her face. Harlem would hop up out of her sleep, hand on her gun and scan the darkness of her bedroom. No one had a clue she was the reason Trill's family and friends were grieving, but it didn't ease her conscious one bit.

As soon as she hopped on the highway, her cell phone rang. Enzo's name flashed across her dashboard, and she rolled her eyes. Answering it on her steering wheel, she sat silently.

"You still on that childish shit I see," Enzo's deep voice rumbled through her speakers.

"What do you want?"

"You know exactly what I want, but you insist on playing with me, huh?"

The smirk on her face crept up on her cheeks before she could stop it. "I'm not playing with you."

"This the first time you answered your phone all week. Lie again," he fussed.

"Do you pay this bill?"

"Nah, but I could've been. I mean, unless you got one of your other niggas paying it," he said with a hint of humor in his tone. Harlem frowned.

"Ha. Right. If one of my niggas is paying anything, it's not my phone bill. Believe that."

"Let you tell it. Where you coming from? Surprised you ain't in jail yet."

Harlem laughed. Enzo had all the jokes today. "Mr. Funny Guy today, huh? What do you want, Enzo before I hang up on you?"

"We need to talk and I'm not telling your ass again."

It was that simple. She could plan a day and time to talk to him right now or he was going to take matters into his own hands. Enzo was tired of playing with her, but more than anything, he was tired of jumping to conclusions about what happened with their child.

"So demanding," she snickered before getting serious. "Can I text you a time and place? I just need a little time."

"Man, you done had five fucking years to—"

Enzo caught himself before he really went the hell off on her. Harlem's eyes blinked rapidly at his outburst. She knew he wasn't playing anymore. It was time to man the hell up and tell the truth.

"I better be receiving a text from you this week. Everything doesn't run on your time, Harlem. I got a life too."

"Yeah... I heard," she replied.

"You heard? You ain't heard shit," Enzo chuckled to calm

his quickened heart rate down. *Did she hear about her?* He questioned to himself. *She couldn't have.*

"I haven't but let me find out some shit. You tripping on me about my past like you don't have one too. I'm not about to be the only one coming clean when we talk, so you better get your story together."

"I'm good, baby. No story to tell. This Eli on the other end so I'ma hit you back."

Harlem smiled, remembering his little brother. She had almost given him and Davion an old fashion butt whoopin' the first time they met.

"Aww, tell him I said hi."

"Hell nah," Enzo laughed. "Y'all not cool, shorty."

"Fuck you."

"Yeah, that's exactly what you need to do when you see me. I miss that pussy but you on punishment, so I'll think about it. Now, bye."

He hung up before Harlem could protest. Smiling, she shook her head. It had been a while since she saw Enzo and she could bet the last thing on his mind would be sex once they sat and talked.

"I guess it's time to face my fears," she breathed out, switching lanes.

CHAPTER THREE

"Oh my gosh," Harlem cooed, grabbing Sailer from Sarena. "She is so pretty."

"Thank you," Sarena replied with a yawn.

It'd been exactly one week since she gave birth to her little angel and she was in love. Marquis insisted on having an at home water birth, and Sarena was so appreciative of his suggestion. It was the most comfortable and gratifying experience ever. She told herself if she were to get pregnant again – which Marquis promised wouldn't be long – she was sticking to water births from home.

"I just love her little self already. When can I take her home?"

Sarena grinned. "You and me both. Don't let Marquis hear you asking that," she giggled. "He'll gladly decline your offer."

Marquis had been in love with Sarena since day one and nothing had changed. His love for her intensified when she became his wife and reached a level he never knew it could reach once she gave birth to their baby girl. He cried real-life tears as she pushed out her five-pound, four ounce body and would have proposed right there had she not already been given his last name.

"Oh Lord," Harlem sighed with a smile. "He has her spoiled already."

"Girl, yes. He took off for the next two weeks, so he could be here with us. I told him he could go in, but you know him."

"Right. Enjoy the help while you can. Are you guys hiring a nanny or anything?" Harlem asked.

Humming for a bit, Sarena shrugged. "Probably not. With the way these babies have been dying at the hands of their caregiver's, I'm terrified of something happening to Sai."

Harlem nodded her head, understanding completely. It seemed like every day she watched the news or scrolled her *Facebook* timeline, a child had loss their life at the hands of someone who was supposed to be watching them. Or, they were murdered. That thought alone sent shivers down her spine. Sailer was good without a nanny for a while.

"It's crazy and sad, girl. How long before you guys head out of town? I don't like that you're taking my baby so soon," Harlem pouted, nestling her face in the crook of Sailer's neck.

It was something about the smell of a newborn that she absolutely loved. They had their own special scent.

"Toward the end of August. So, a little over a month away. I may stay for a few more months and just meet him there."

Harlem gave her the side eye and a smirk. "Now you know he's not going to like that."

"I know, but my mama's already scolded me about taking her grandbaby away so soon. Talking about 'Just wait until she's six months,' but that's too long. I'll give her two and I'm out." Sarena laughed.

"Well, I'll definitely have to come visit. Sweden seems like a nice place to visit."

"Yes. You and Enzo will have to visit us," Sarena said, sneakily eyeing her friend. "How are things with you two?"

Harlem sighed. Things were how they'd been since she last spoke to him. Tense. They hadn't got the chance to sit and talk yet. Though she said she would text him, Harlem had done everything but reach out to Enzo. He was running on a short fuse with her stubbornness; if it could even be considered that anymore.

"Considering the circumstances... they could be better."

"Is that your doing or his?"

Harlem rolled her eyes. Sarena had always been the rational friend. Rather than looking at situations from one person's perspective, she always tried to see the bigger picture from all parties involved. She knew her friend was being stubborn, but what she really wanted to know was why? Enzo had been extremely patient, and Harlem knew that. She just didn't feel like bringing up the past.

"Honestly, both of ours. Solely me, but whatever," she snickered as Sailer yet out a yawn and peeled her eyes open.

Staring down at her, Harlem got a little emotional. She always wondered what she and Enzo's child would have looked like. As handsome as he was, Harlem wanted a replica of him in baby form. She smiled a little when Sailer's little lips poked out as if she were ready to eat.

"Someone's hungry."

"Again," Sarena chuckled. "She'll be back sleep in no time."

"Auntie loves you, Sailer boo."

Handing her back to Sarena, she positioned herself to breastfeed just as Marquis walked in scratching his beard. Looking up at her husband, Sarena's eyes glossed over in an array of emotions. The most potent one being love. It was the strongest emotion known to mankind, and she thanked God every day for blessing her with a man who openly showed her what it really felt like to be loved.

"What up, Harlem," he spoke as Harlem stood to her feet to hug him.

"Not much. You have a beauty on your hands, sir," she laughed.

Marquis shook his head and smiled. "Man. Don't remind me. I swear she looks just like her fine ass mama."

"Marquis," Sarena hissed.

"Look," he chuckled. "You about to get me in trouble already. I just woke up."

"My fault. You know I mean no harm," Harlem replied with a chuckle.

Stepping over to Sarena, Marquis gave her a kiss on the lips before taking ahold of Sailer's hand. Her tiny fingers wrapped around his and her big, bright eyes stared up at him like she knew exactly who he was; and she did.

"Hey, daddy's baby. You hungry, huh?"

Harlem blinked back tears at the scene before her and smiled when Sarena looked her way. This is what she envisioned for she and Enzo. The married life with a child or a few calling her mommy. Living their dreams out and spending the rest of their lives together. The only dreams Harlem had back then were of surviving. For so long, that's all she set out to do. School was an option at one point, but life got in the way as it seemed to have been doing since she was born.

"Please be sure to send me pictures when you guys take them," she said and Sarena nodded.

"Of course, boo. She's scheduled for next week with Onna."

"She's a beast behind the camera," Harlem praised. "Let me go. I'll FaceTime y'all later on."

"Okay. Babe, walk her out for me?"

Marquis nodded, and they headed to the front door. Congratulating him once more, Harlem climbed in her truck and prepared to make the thirty-minute drive home. Playing no music, she drove in silence, but her thoughts were louder than ever. She was so deep in them when her phone rang over the Bluetooth system, she jumped and sucked her teeth. Pressing the button on her steering wheel, she answered Yaz' call.

"What's up, hoe!" Yaz said animatedly.

She's in a good mood. "Nothing. What's up?"

Yaz frowned. "Un, un. What the hell is wrong with you?"

Harlem chuckled and shook her head. "Nothing. I was just in deep thought until you called me."

"Mhm. Where you coming from or headed to? I know you in the car."

"You are too nosy for me. I'm about to pull up at home. I just left from seeing Sailer."

Yaz sucked her teeth. "You went over there without me? You ain't real, man."

Laughing, Harlem said, "Whatever. You be acting like you hate making the drive, so I wasn't about to wait around for you. I'll send you some pictures. She's so damn pretty."

"I know, hoe. I saw her the day she was born. Send me some pictures anyway."

"I will. What you up to?"

"Girl," Yaz dragged. "Junior nem' want me to dance for this little party."

Harlem scrunched her face up. "Who the hell is Junior and dance? Dance like what?"

"You know... stripping. I'm just going to dance that's all," Yaz said, holding back her laugh.

"You ain't no- wait! I can't stand you," Harlem hissed with a laugh. "Junior better take his ass on. Ronnie and Tricks too."

Yaz was cackling on the other end. Harlem was so deep in thought; she almost missed the *Player's Club* references Yaz was acting out.

"You were really about to go in on me."

Harlem chuckled. "I was. You play too much."

Pulling up to her house, her heart dropped to her feet when she saw Enzo's car parked in her driveway. The days of ducking and dodging him were over. Licking her lips, Harlem felt her stomach getting queasy as if she had to throw up. Her mouth watered thinking of him just sitting in her crib waiting for her.

"Harlem!" Yaz yelled out, making her damn near jump out of her skin.

"What!"

"Don't make me come over there. You're acting strange."

"I'm fine. It's just Enzo is over here, girl," she said, opening her garage.

She tried peeking into his car as she slowly pulled into her driveway, but there was no need. Powering his car off with a press of a button, Enzo opened his car door and stepped out, greeting her needy eyes. Tugging on the band of his sweats, he pulled them up and leaned against his car. He hadn't been waiting for long, but it was long enough.

"Humph," Yaz breathed out. "Serves your ass right. Call me later and let me know how it goes. Love you."

"Love you too," Harlem mumbled as the line disconnected.

Sighing, she cut her truck off, grabbed her purse from the passenger side and climbed out. Walking around to the front of the truck, she hit the lock button and eyed Enzo's get up for the day. He made sweats and a plain white v-neck look damn good. When he brushed a hand down his thick head of hair, Harlem rolled her eyes.

Why the hell did he decide to come over here looking so good?

"What up, though?" He spoke, pushing himself off the car and walking her way.

Harlem swallowed hard. "Nothing. What's up?"

"You already know why I'm here."

"Of course, I do. I'm shocked you didn't invite yourself in," she said, brushing past him and entering the garage.

Trekking behind her, Enzo smirked. He could have, but he decided not to. "Nah. I ain't know if your man was inside or not."

Harlem quickly turned to face him with a mug on her face. "Here you go with the bullshit already."

"I'm just saying. You know how you do. Having niggas

pay bills and shit. Ain't that what you said?" he replied as the garage door closed and they entered the house.

Ignoring him, Harlem punched in her six-digit code, disarmed her alarm and tossed her purse onto the countertop. Opening the fridge, she pulled out a bottle of wine, grabbed the largest wine glass she had in her cabinet, and poured a generous amount. Enzo's left brow lifted as she guzzled majority of it down in seconds.

"Stressful day?" he questioned.

"Nope, but I needed this before you began to work my nerves."

"A nigga stress you that much, I cause you to drink?"

That question and assumption couldn't be any truer and he had no clue. Closing the fridge, she walked off with her wine glass in hand toward the living room. Releasing a deep sigh, Enzo followed behind her. Sitting across from her on the loveseat, he got comfortable as he watched Harlem slip her shoes off and sit down. Her slow movements told him she was trying to prolong their conversation, but it was too late.

"You don't cause me to drink. Not anymore, I should say," she finally replied, sitting her wine glass down on the coaster.

Enzo cleared his throat at her revelation. *Damn, am I ready for whatever she about to tell me?* He had to question himself for a second. Being the cause of Harlem's pain in the first place had him fucked up for so long, he'd hate to go back down this road and not regain her trust. He loved her, there was no denying that, but he'd let her be if she told him today that she was better off without him. He saw firsthand how sticking around for the sake of love turned out. His mama was living proof.

"So, back then... that's all you did when I left?"

"While I was in school, yes. But that part of my life was short-lived. I wasn't built to be a college girl," she snickered.

"You could've been, still can be."

"Nah. That ship has sailed. Too many bad memories honestly."

Enzo nodded, but told himself he'd bring it back up later on. He knew she wanted nothing more than to go away for school, but circumstances back then caused her to return home before she could really enjoy the college experience.

"Speaking of memories... what's up with this baby you claimed was mine?"

Picking her glass up, she took two gulps and sat it back down. "Straight to it, huh?" She chuckled to mask her nervousness, but it didn't help. "The baby was yours. I wasn't out here fucking niggas raw like you claimed. Let alone letting them nut in me."

"I ain't mean to disrespect you like that, but you had a nigga hot for real."

"I know, but don't ever disrespect me like that again. I don't play that shit," she said seriously, staring him dead in the eyes.

"You got it, ma. I see you checking me," he chuckled.

"Now, go ahead. Tell me what's up. Did you know before I left?"

Harlem shook her head no. "No. I didn't find out until a month after you left.

By that time, you had changed your number I guess. I don't know. You wouldn't return any of my calls or texts or anything. I felt so alone."

When she sniffled, Enzo wanted to get up and go hug her, but he forced himself to remain seated. Harlem needed to let this all out. He knew she hadn't brought it up to anyone because that's just how she was. She held shit in, especially shit that couldn't change. Bottling her emotions over the years had toughened her up and made her somewhat disconnected with the softer side of her. The feminine side. When they did spill out, it was in anger.

"How far along were you?" he asked.

"Nine weeks."

"Damn," Enzo mumbled shaking his head. "Did you get an abortion or what?"

Harlem looked up at him with tear-filled eyes. "I should have. Don't look like that. Let me tell you how it all went down, please. Just... hear me out."

Enzo's nose flared, but he sat back and nodded for her to continue. "Aight."

Taking a deep breath, Harlem thought back to the day she found out she was pregnant. It was one of the most terrifying, and overwhelming moments of her life.

"I have to tell him," Harlem whispered lowly.

Staring down at the pregnancy tests on the counter, all three showed thick, double pink lines. She couldn't believe her eyes. Her vision became cloudy just thinking about her carrying his child.

"Awww, boo," Sarena cooed.

"You ain't gotta tell his ass shit," Yaz hissed.

She loved her friend, and the way Enzo did her was straight up wrong in her eyes. With her not having a father figure in her life, Yaz was prepared to run the lecture her mother gave her down to Harlem about not needing the father in her child's life.

"Stop, Yaz. This is his baby just as much as it is hers."

Yaz sucked her teeth and rolled her eyes hard. "Whatever. Had that nigga stayed, he'd know what the fuck was up. I don't like him."

Zoned out, Harlem ignored their bantering behind her. She was in utter disbelief at the news. Granted, she and Enzo had been sexing like the horny in love teenagers they were right before he left, but Harlem never once thought she'd end up pregnant.

While away at school, she didn't feel like herself and when the first opportunity to come home presented itself, she did. Yaz had been the one to point out her belly, but Harlem had chucked it up to her already gaining her Freshmen 15. That wasn't the case at all. While Yaz' mama was at work, the girls drove Sarena's car to CVS and picked up three pregnancy tests. Finding out she was carrying a child was not the type of weekend Harlem had in mind.

"What're you going to do?" Sarena asked.

"I don't know. Should I call him again?"

Harlem had never felt so indecisive in her life. She was fresh into what heartbreak felt like, dealing with Andrea and the drama Dre had caused in their life, and now she was pregnant. The support and reassurance from her friends was needed more than ever.

"I think you should," Sarena voiced.

"I don't care. Just know, regardless if he's here or not, we got you," was Yaz' reply.

Blinking back tears, Harlem nodded her head, and they filed out of the bathroom. Pacing Yaz' bedroom floor, Harlem's heart raced, and her nervousness rocketed to another level as the phone rang loudly in her ear. After the sixth ring, it went to voicemail. Sighing, she looked up at her friends.

"He didn't answer."

"Call back," Sarena suggested softly.

Yaz just sucked her teeth. Exhaling, Harlem dialed Enzo's number again. Ducked off at his cousin Grady's crib, Enzo looked down at his ringing phone. Seeing Harlem's name with a heart emoji by it, for the second time within a minute, had him shaking his head before he declined her call.

"Who calls you screening?" Huss asked, looking over at him.

Enzo looked up and said, "My shorty's. I just need to get my number changed."

"That's your shorty but you ignoring her calls?" Grady asked, confused. His girl would blow his line down if he sent her to voicemail.

"It's complicated, man. Y'all know that."

"And you only making shit worse by ignoring her. Trust me," Huss told him.

Enzo knew he probably was, but the damage had already been done. Answering her phones calls would only make things worse in his opinion. Staring down at her phone, Harlem frowned when it went to voicemail quicker than the first time.

"Maybe he's busy," Sarena said.

"He ain't no fucking busy. Look," Yaz said, going to stand in front of Harlem. "We got you okay? Fuck Enzo. If he calls back, tell him. If not, you have all the support you need until he gets his mind right. Don't ever feel like you need him, aight?"

"B-But I do," Harlem said lowly, as warm tears coated her cheeks. "I need him so bad. This isn't fair."

When she sat down and cried in her hands, Yaz looked at Sarena and threw her hands up. She promised to be there for Harlem but seeing this soft side of her was baffling. Harlem had always been the tough girl. The one who got shit done and handled by any means necessary, so to see her breaking down over a nigga had Yaz perplexed. Rubbing her back, Sarena sent a silent prayer up for her friend because Lord knows she needed it.

With Enzo not replying to any of her texts, and soon finding out a few days later that he changed his number, Harlem fell into a deep depression. Her mini vacation home had ended and she was back at school with onerous thoughts of getting an abortion on her mind. Peeking over her shoulder in the school library, she checked to see if anyone was behind her before searching for abortion options on the internet. Immediately, tons of resources, articles, and definitions of the word surfaced.

For hours, Harlem sat and researched her options. The risks of getting an abortion, how likely it was to survive, the size her baby was and a plethora of things her mind couldn't shake. She didn't make her mind up that day, but she did schedule an appointment with a nearby pregnancy center. After finding out she was nine weeks along and seeing her tiny baby on the monitor, Harlem immediately erased all thoughts of getting an abortion from her mental. Regardless if Enzo was a part of its life, she vowed to cherish her unborn and smother it with nothing but love. In the end, that's how it was created.

Excited for the new life she was carrying, Harlem stopped by Dollar General and picked out a small teddy bear for her baby. It'd be its first from the mommy to be. She sent Yaz and

Sarena a picture of it, she was so happy. But, in Harlem's world, happy endings never seemed to happen.

Not even three days after she visited the clinic, Harlem woke up to severe stomach cramps. Feeling the dampness on her sheets, she frowned, lifted the covers and used her phone's flashlight to see what was going on down there. A large, dark red blood puddle covered her white sheets. Telling herself not to panic, she slowly, on trembling legs, climbed from her twin sized bed. Gathering a fresh set of clothing and undergarments, Harlem made her way to the community bathroom down the hall after wrapping herself in a robe.

In the shower, her cramps didn't stop nor did the bleeding, but she told herself not to panic. When she was back in her room, she put on an overnight pad, stripped the bed of its linen, wiped the mattress down, and placed fresh sheets on the bed. For the next thirty minutes, she googled questions as to why she may have been bleeding. When she scared herself to the point tears were in her eyes, she decided to call it a night, but frowned when she felt the heaviness of her pad and the coldness of her body.

Within thirty minutes, she had bled through an overnight pad, which is thicker in layers than a normal one. Terrified of something extremely wrong, she struggled to stand to her feet. The room began to spin, and everything seemed to get darker. Her entire frame shook as she reached for her phone. Tears spilled from her eyes as her hearing became cloudy and before she could dial 911, she collapsed on the cold tile floor in her *dorm room. Harlem was passed out and quickly losing oxygen, and had her roommate not shown up ten minutes later, she would have lost her life.*

Though the doctors explained the amount of blood she lost was due to hemorrhaging, Harlem was too distraught to process what it meant and why it had happened. Her blood pressure had dropped, and her hemoglobin levels were in the single digits. By the grace of God, she had survived, and she had her roommate to thank. ..."

Not bothering to wipe the tears from her face, Harlem stared at Enzo with pleading eyes for him to say something. He had tears in his and he had to briefly close them to gather himself. Biting down on his bottom lip, Enzo placed a fist under his nose and exhaled deeply. His heart was aching for Harlem. Hearing her tell what happened and getting choked up in between all the details had him feeling like the biggest asshole in life.

"I-It was so hard for me to bounce back," Harlem choked out. "So fucking hard. I wanted to drop out of school so bad first semester, but instead, I stuck it out cause' that's what I do. I get through shit."

She paused and shook her head.

"Not this, though. I didn't get through this for a while. I started drinking heavily. Skipping classes because I was either too hungover or I decided to drink instead. I hated being at school. I had no support, Enzo! No one! Everyone I needed the most was here in Kansas City. So, yes. At the time after everything happened, I thought maybe getting an abortion would have saved me from all the trauma and pain I went through from having a miscarriage. I could have d-died," she cried.

Standing to his feet, Enzo swooped her up in his arms and held her tightly. Tears gathered in his eyes as she cried her heart out into his chest.

"I needed you. I fucking needed you and you left me."

"I know, baby. I'm so fucking sorry. I swear to God I am."

Harlem had held this cry in for years. This was her first time admitting to anyone that she wanted to get an abortion because she didn't want to be judged. Enough shit had transpired in her life to where she had to explain how she ended up where she was, deciding to get an abortion wasn't one she wanted to add to the list of explanations so she kept quiet.

When her cries quieted, Enzo loosened the hold he had on her but didn't let her go. Staring down at her tearstained face, his heart was palpitating with remorse. Pressing his forehead against hers, he kissed the tip of her nose and exhaled.

"I'm so sorry you went through all of that alone, baby."

Harlem sniffled. "It's fine. I mean, it's over now."

"Nah. Don't say it's fine because you think that's what you need to say. I get it. I fucked up for leaving you but was even more in the wrong for ghosting you like I did. You ain't deserve that, and I swear I'll make it up to you for however long you need me to."

Swallowing hard, Harlem shook her head no. She didn't want to depend on him to help close up a wound he reopened. Yes, having this conversation with him stung badly, but not to the point where she wanted to sulk in the past about it. Her depressive days had been long gone. The nights she stayed up crying, wishing he was there to hold her close and tell her everything would be okay were over. Harlem had overcome her losses and they were now lessons she learned.

"No, really. It's fine, Enzo. You did what you had to do, and I did what I had to do. I did fault you for a while, but there was nothing either of us could have done honestly," she said, softly clearing her throat.

The thought of having to find out Harlem had died from undergoing a miscarriage and he not being there, was eating Enzo up inside. All those years he stayed away didn't seem to hold any value at the moment. He swore if he could reverse the hands of time, he'd stay.

"I could have been there," he griped, squeezing her hands.

"Yeah, well that's just something you'll have to live with. This is why I didn't want to tell you. I mean eventually, I knew I was going to have to, but not this soon."

"I can't lie, Harlem; I'm fucked up behind what you went through. Where was your mama when all this went down?"

Harlem rolled her eyes and sat down on the couch. "She

was there, physically. Mentally? I couldn't tell you. She was sad, but she had been more depressed over losing Dre than anything. I guess her daughter about to lose her life wasn't as important," she replied with a shrug.

This was the first time either of them had brought up Dre's name since that dreadful night. The night that had changed their lives forever. The buzz behind his death had died down, and Enzo was grateful for that. After the bomb Harlem had just dropped on him, he knew dealing with anything else at the moment would surely cause him to lose his cool.

"Damn. And all of this happened because his ass," Enzo huffed.

"Technically, this happened because you nutted in me," she replied, lightening the mood some.

They both grinned at one another and Enzo shook his head. "Man. We were fucking like crazy before I dipped out of town."

"Exactly. Not pulling out or anything."

"Nah. I did like once," he threw in and Harlem sucked her teeth.

"Compared to all the other times, that one time didn't count clearly," she chuckled, wiping her eye.

The two grew quiet for a minute, relishing in their own thoughts. Harlem was thinking how lighter she felt now that she had that off her chest. Enzo, on the other hand, was thinking how they could get back to focusing on them and starting fresh.

"So."

"I just–"

They both began and chuckled lowly. Enzo nodded his head, silently telling her to go ahead.

"So. What secrets do you have to share?"

"Secrets? None at all."

Harlem cocked her head to the side. "You sure about that?"

"Positive."

"So you weren't down in Detroit showing out while you were away?"

Enzo chuckled. "I don't know what you consider showing out, but I don't have anything to hide. For real."

"Besides that chick who was at Lucci's house, you didn't fool with any other women?" Harlem asked, trying to see what he had really been on in the 'D' besides getting money.

"Ah. So, that's what you want to know. If I had a woman down there?"

"No. I want to know should I be concerned about another female trying to come to me, woman to woman. We have history, so our bond is a little special. At least to me, it is."

"It is," he added.

"And, I don't want there to be any confusion, if for some reason, you have a female ducked off in Detroit who thinks she's going to get an explanation as to why we are as close as we are. We're not in a relationship, but I'd like to eventually be in one."

"With me?" Enzo had to question.

"Yes, with you. Who the hell else?"

He chuckled lowly at the bass in her voice. "Aye. I'm just trying to make sure I understand what you sayin'. So, basically, you want to know if I'm entertaining another female besides you before we try and take things to the next level?"

Harlem nodded her head yes. "Correct."

Enzo brushed a hand down his head. He had every intention to keep his life in Detroit separate from the one he had in Kansas City, but that was starting to look like a not so easy task. Lying to Harlem wasn't the best option either. He knew after this conversation if she really wanted to find some shit out, she would. That simple.

"I wouldn't call it entertaining," Enzo started, and Harlem's eyes bucked. "I'm cool with a female though."

"Cool as in y'all friends and fuck from time to time, or cool as in, she count up your money, meet your niggas, got a key to your crib and know the passcode to your phone, cool?"

She needed him to be specific on the details of his involvement with whoever this woman was. Harlem wasn't in the business of entertaining a nigga who had a woman. In fact, she'd turned down several licks because the men were too caught up in their female companions and she needed their full attention to be on her.

"You asking questions as if you don't have an ex who be blowing your line down," Enzo voiced.

"Exactly. Kartel is an ex, not someone I'm entertaining, let alone fucking. You've been laying up with me for the last couple of months, so you should already know there's nothing between us."

"And during all them months, have I been entertaining another female? Nah, don't look like that. You asking me questions, I can do the same."

Harlem rolled her eyes. "Honestly, I never even paid *that* much attention. But, now that it's been brought to my attention, you do go missing for some days. You know what that means?"

"Nah. Tell me what it means, shorty, since you got all the answers in the world," Enzo chuckled.

"That you are keeping something a secret, or you just like to go missing. One or the other."

"'Cause if a nigga doesn't talk to you for two days there's another woman involved, huh?"

Harlem picked her wine glass up and swallowed the last sip. "What other reason would you need to go two days without talking to me? I mean, unless the bitch is a lick then I'd somewhat understand."

Laughing, Enzo shook his head. Only Harlem would say some wild shit like that.

"She ain't no lick, man."

"Oh," she chirped, interested now piqued. "So, there is a *she*?"

Harlem was honestly surprised Enzo hadn't lied. She never put him out to be a liar nor was he one. There was no use in lying.

Giving her a subtle nod, Enzo replied, "Yeah. Somethin' like that."

"Hmm. Interesting. And here you were sweating me over Trill."

"'Cause you really caught feelings for that nigga on some weird shit," he scoffed, feeling himself getting angry all over again.

"For your information, I already had somewhat of a relationship with him."

Enzo sucked his teeth and waved her off. "You wasn't fucking with him like *that*. Not until I rolled up on you at the strip club."

Harlem wasn't even surprised that he had peeped her moves that night. Enzo had only noticed the two talking because he and his crew were there scoping him out as well. He peeped when Harlem went to the restroom; Trill was right behind her. Being the type of fine Harlem was, he already knew she wasn't fucking with no lame who didn't have some money to his name and Trill had plenty.

"Stalking ass," she huffed playfully.

"Aye. I'm just well aware of my surroundings, shorty. You know that. On a serious note though, I'm proud of you. You bounced back from a lot of shit most people wouldn't have. I can tell you really don't trust my word anymore, but know I always got you."

Harlem was confused as to why Enzo was saying all of this. Granted, it felt good to hear him say he was proud of her, but for what? She had to get out here and get it just like he had to. The way she was living wasn't one she wished upon anyone. It kept her up at night, filled with guilt, and hating the life she had made for herself. There wasn't shit to be proud of, unless he meant doing it without him. In that case, Harlem was going to do that regardless. No nigga would ever stop her from eating.

"Why are you saying all of this? You must be leaving again," she said dryly.

Enzo scratched his head. "Yeah. For a little bit. Tie up some loose ends back in Detroit. I'll be back though."

"Okay. Enjoy your trip."

Drawing his head back, Enzo's face slightly contorted in surprise. "That's it? No cursing me out?"

"Nah. You got a life, too, right?" Harlem questioned as her phone rang loudly from the kitchen.

Standing to her feet, she left Enzo in his thoughts and went to answer her phone. Pulling it from her purse, she saw it was Kartel calling, and she smirked. Normally, Harlem would have ignored his call and shot him a text, but not today. Oh no. Today, she was about to answer his call. To keep it one hundred, she was feeling a way about Enzo having a so-called woman back in Detroit, but she didn't show it. She was skilled in the area of not wearing her heart on her sleeve anymore. Answering the phone, she turned the volume up and walked back into the living room.

"You must be in a good mood," Kartel said with a grin on his face.

Smirking, Harlem rolled her eyes. "Possibly. What's going on?"

"Shit. Trying to come see you. Rap with you for a little minute."

Hearing a male's voice through her speakers, Enzo frowned at her and shook his head. Harlem looked him dead in his face before replying to Kartel.

"Come through in about an hour. Bring me some food too."

Kartel chuckled. "Aight. I got you."

"I didn't tell you what I wanted, though."

"You ain't have to. I know you, but text it to me anyway like I know you gon' do."

Harlem smiled. He did know her very well. "Okay. See you in an hour."

"Aight."

Hanging up the phone, she sat it on the table, and Enzo picked it right up. He didn't give a fuck. Going to her call log, he sucked his teeth and was ready to dial Kartel back and tell that nigga if he pulled up over there, he was gone have to see him, but instead, he just tossed her phone on the couch.

"You bold as fuck, shorty. On me."

"Here you fucking go. We are not a couple."

"So what. Out of respect don't be answering no other nigga's phone call when I'm in your presence. Straight up."

"Respect?" She hissed, cocking her head back. "You in my mothafuckin' house."

Enzo was taken aback by the grit in her tone. *Oh, she's serious now*. He could only nod his head, seeing as though she had a point.

"Aight. You got that, Harlem. I'm bout' to shake for I have to catch a body in this bitch."

"Whatever, nigga. Leave like you always do."

"Aye," he hissed, turning back around. "You got somethin' you wanna say to me? Some shit you wanna get off yo' chest? Cause' I ain't feeling what you just said. We not about to keep going over the same shit. We both know why I left. The past is the past. Let that shit go."

"The past is only the past to you because you moved the fuck on, unbothered. You don't have to look in the eyes of the people you hurt the most because of your past and see their pain. So, don't tell me to let shit go and basically get over it if you aren't willing to help me get through it. If I should be letting anything go, it's you."

Clenching his jaw, Enzo stepped over to where she was sitting and bent down until he was eye level with her. "Well, that ain't a mothafuckin' option. If you wanted me to move on for good, that's too damn bad 'cause I'm here to stay, shorty. Ain't no getting rid of me."

Grabbing her chin with force, Enzo kissed her pouty lips before gently mushing her head back. He was pissed that she kept trying to throw him leaving in his face, but he promised today would be the last time. Backing away from her with a mug on his face, he pulled the door open and walked out with ease. Fuming, with butterflies swarming her belly, Harlem sucked on her bottom lip, savoring the feel of his plush lips.

"I can't stand his fine ass," she huffed.

Harlem and Enzo were both upset, but not to the point where it would hinder their relationship after today. In fact, their conversation was much needed on both ends. It gave Enzo the clarity he needed on how to move on with her and it gave Harlem a sense of freedom now that her secret was out. Where their relationship went after this, was solely up to them.

CHAPTER FOUR

"Baby, I'ma be home in a few hours, tops. Man quit playing with me, Makiya," Grady chuckled at his fiancée. She stayed with the bullshit. "Yeah. You know a nigga loves you more. Yeah. Aight."

With a shake of his head, Grady locked his phone and slid it into his pants pocket. Huss had a smirk on his face seeing his boy all in love, but it was a good look.

"She got that shit on lock, huh?" Enzo asked playfully.

"You already know. Now, back to what I was saying."

"Nigga, what I was saying," Huss interrupted. "The only thing you were trying to tell him was how to get locked the fuck up."

Enzo had landed in Detroit earlier that morning, and after running errands and getting a nap in, he was chilling back with his folks at *A Hustler's Spot*. Grady and Huss had opened the club a few years back, and business hadn't fell off since. It was one of the most well-known nightclub in the city and drew in big crowds, mostly every weekend.

Though his cousin had started out in the drug game and scaled back some, Enzo knew that wasn't the route he wanted to take in life. He'd leave that up to Lucci. Scamming wasn't going out of style, but he was tired of doing it. At the rate he was going, if he were to ever get caught, they'd throw the book at him for sure.

"Whatever," Grady said dismissively.

"You gotta find something you good at and expand on that shit," Huss explained. "Not just for the money either. What can you see yourself doing every day you wake up?"

For a minute, Enzo thought about his question. Scamming had been his means of survival for so long, he honestly didn't have an answer. Making money was what he enjoyed doing; how he was getting it is what needed to change. Frustrated, he sucked his teeth.

"I don't know, man. Maybe this going legit shit ain't for me."

"It ain't for you right now because you're not applying yourself," Grady added. "Could you see yourself running a club?"

"It don't seem that bad, but I'd have to be in a position to test it out."

Huss nodded his head as the wheels in his head began to

turn. "I'ma hook you up with this nigga back in KC who owns a few lounges."

"Aw yeah. That nigga Juvie," Grady said.

"Him too, but I was talking about Meechi. He an OG in this shit and could really lace you with some game since you ain't trying to hear us."

"Nah. I hear y'all. It's just a lot to process. You niggas acting like y'all went strictly legit."

Grady smirked. He was pushing weight out the basement of his late grandfather's gas stations that they owned before he went almost completely legit. Drugs were still being sold in the club, but not how it used to.

"We never said we did. We just thought and moved smarter. You catch a federal charge behind the shit you into, and it's a wrap, Enzo. Straight up."

Huss nodded looking up from his emails. "Just think about it. I'll shoot Juvie a text with yo' number so y'all can link when you touch back down."

"Bet. Good lookin'. I'm only gone be here for about a week tops. Got some shit I need to handle."

"She one of them?" Grady said, pointing to one of the TV's that was monitoring the club.

Standing to his feet, Enzo squinted his eyes at one of the main reasons he had flew back in town. Licking his lips, Enzo nodded his head. Chasney Davidson had somehow snuck her way into his life and hadn't made an exit since, but he felt it was time to.

"Yep. Hope her ass don't be on no crazy shit. I ain't with all that."

"Shiiit," Grady dragged with a chuckle. "You better be with it today. You know you spoiled her ass."

Enzo shook his head. "Don't remind me. Let me get down here," he said, extending his arm so they could slap hands. Walking over to Huss, he did the same. "I'll hit y'all up so we can link before I head out."

"Aight, fool. Be safe. You better make sure you visit grandma too," Grady told him.

"Fasho. I need a pan of macaroni for the road," Enzo chuckled, pulling the door open.

Instead of taking the steps down, he hopped on the elevator to give him time to think about how he was going to break the news to Chasney. She was what Enzo considered a good girl. He hadn't quite turned her out like he had done Harlem. They had been fooling around for the past two years, and had his heart not belonged to Harlem, his baby, he would have wifed Chasney. The ding brought him back to reality and he climbed off, heading her way.

From the back, Chasney's beautiful chocolate skin was on display in the top that had her entire back out. Her jeans sat low on her tiny hips, a pair of clear heels were on her feet, and her hair was styled in braids that were wrapped in a bun. She was sexy and the lights bouncing off her creamy, dark skin had Enzo licking his lips. Glancing toward the bar, Enzo tossed Duffie, the head bartender, a head nod.

Chasney's friend, Dia saw Enzo approaching and she grinned.

Wrapping his arm around Chasney's midsection, Enzo whispered, "You look good."

Knowing that voice and scent of cologne from anywhere, Chasney grinned before spinning around slowly. "Hi, babe," she cooed.

Her bright smile made Enzo grin. Chasney's dark brown eyes were lit up and always did when Enzo was in her presence.

"What's up with it."

"Nothing much. Just came to have a few drinks with D."

Enzo nodded her way. "That's what's up."

"I didn't know you were back in town. When did you get here?"

"Like an hour ago," Enzo lied to save face. "Was gon' hit your line when I left from here, but here you are."

Chasney smirked. "Yes, here I am. Wanna have drinks with us?"

"Nah. I'ma have to pass. Drink on me though," he said, pulling some money out of his pocket and handed it to her.

"I can leave with you. Go back to my place? I missed you," Chasney whispered lustfully. She already had a few shots up in her. The gloss of her eyes was a dead giveaway.

"Stay and kick it with your girl. I'ma head to the crib. Slide through when you leave here."

Chasney grabbed his hand. "You sure?"

Kissing her cheek, Enzo nodded. "Positive. Enjoy your night."

With squinted eyes, Chasney gave him a once over but said okay. When Enzo walked away, Dia looked at her friend with her lips tooted up.

"What?" Chasney pressed.

"Nothing, girl. Nothing at all."

Dia kept what she was thinking to herself. When Chasney first met Enzo, she fell hard for him in weeks, and her friend had warned her about Enzo's type. Yes, he was a gentleman, respectful, and spoiled the fuck out of her, but he'd also break her heart with a blink of an eye. She just hoped her girl had listened those years back because she could feel something between them was off.

Deep down, Chasney felt it too. After not seeing Enzo for so long, she expected him to be all over her. The kiss to the cheek, instead of the sensual lip lock they normally engaged in was proof that something or someone had his mind preoccupied. And, that someone was Harlem.

In his car, Enzo pulled his phone out of his pocket just as a FaceTime call from Harlem came through. It was dark out, but the lighting from outside gave his walnut-golden skin color a dark shadow that had Harlem biting down on her bottom lip once the call connected.

Enzo brushed a hand down his waves and smirked. "Harlem."

"Enzo," she replied, smiling. "Where are you?"

"Headed to my crib. What you on?"

"In the bed chilling. I didn't want anything, just wanted to check on you. See how your little trip went."

Enzo chuckled. They hadn't spoke in a few days and Harlem no longer cared that he had gone missing now that she knew why. She really just wanted to see if he made it safely. Plus, the nightmare she just had awakened her from her sleep and had her slightly shook. Enzo seemed to be the only one who could put her rattling nerves at ease with just the sound of his voice.

"I just got here this morning. What? You miss me already?" he chuckled.

Harlem rolled her eyes. "Yeah right. I had a... a crazy ass dream. Shit felt so real, I just had to call you."

"Word? What was it about?"

Clearing her throat, she shook her head. "Someone was following me. I don't know how they saw me though. A black mask covered their entire face. Me and you were in the car together, and they rolled up on us and shot you in the head," she said, swallowing hard.

"Damn," Enzo breathed out. He was not expecting that.

"Right. Crazy thing is when I went to cradle your body, it wasn't your face. It was Trill's."

"The fuck?"

"Right. It was so weird. So fucking creepy. I woke up sweating and shit," she said, shaking her head.

Enzo was stuck. That wasn't the type of dream he wanted

Harlem to be having, but he knew it came with the life they lived. For the first year after he killed Dre, he had similar dreams. Taking someone's life wasn't for the faint of heart. Though his was out of self-defense, it still haunted him.

"Damn, baby. I'ont even know what to say. You in the bed early. It's only nine there."

"I was tired."

"I'm starting to think you don't really have a job," he laughed.

"I did, but not anymore. I haven't worked there in two weeks."

"That's why you be having so much time on your hands. When I get back, we need to talk about other living options."

Harlem's eyebrow lifted. "Living options? Nigga, you not moving with me."

"I can if I wanted to, but not that. I'm talking about what we do for a living. I think you should get back in school."

"Um, yeah, no. Not happening," she said, yawning.

"Why not?"

"Because. What would I even go to school for, Enzo? I've been out for too long."

Enzo shook his head. "Nah. It's all in your head, baby. It's cool though. I won't be home until next week, so you got time to think."

"My mind is already made up. Your *woman* only making you stay for a week? Hmm. She must not have that on lock," she snickered.

Enzo couldn't help but chuckle at her jealousy. It was a side of Harlem he hadn't got a chance to witness yet, and he found it amusing. Cute even. She was subtle with her shade but throwing it nonetheless.

"We ain't talking about her. We talking about us. Like I said, be ready to discuss some shit when I touch down."

"I might be out with my nigga when you get here, so I'll let you know when I'm available."

Enzo's jaw tightened. "Keep on playin' with me. That nigga gon' come up missing."

"And so is the bitch you down there pacifying. You think you the only one with connections?" she asked, cocking her head to the side. "Keep playing with me if you want to."

"Nah," he said with a shake of his head. "What happened to all that 'We aren't together Enzo' bullshit you were spitting?"

"We still aren't but don't think you about to be calling shots with shit, unless I can do the same."

"Yeah, yeah. I hear you, shorty. What's up with ol' girl?"

Enzo didn't have to say her name for Harlem to know who she was talking about. That was the reason Harlem was tired. Zeema was indeed pregnant, and she had been over Vonzell's honeycomb hideout much longer than she intended to today. The girl who came and patched Harlem up after Enzo shot her did such a good job and was so professional, Harlem got her number for future incidents. Her number came in handy today and she confirmed that Zeema was with child.

It was eating Harlem alive to know who her child's father was, and that was the only reason she hadn't killed her yet. Her fate was still up in the air honestly. After that dream she just had, Harlem was thinking about letting her go for good. Zeema snitching would incriminate herself, so snitching wouldn't be the best option. Her decision hadn't been set in stone yet, though.

"She good. We're good," she said, getting to the point.

"Aight. I'ma trust you on that. Call me when you wake up in the morning."

"No. I'm not gon' feel all mushy and wanna talk to you tomorrow, so don't call me 'cause I'm going to ignore you."

Enzo laughed at how quickly she just switched up on him. "You must be about to start your period. Moody fucking girl. I love you," he said, meaning every word. His thick vocal chords made Harlem's pussy and heart throb in sync.

"I love you too, with your sneaky ass. Got a whole bitch out of town and ain't once mentioned her. Bye. You just pissed me off."

Before Enzo could reply, Harlem hung up in his face. Chuckling, Enzo shook his head with a smile on his face. Pulling out of the parking lot, Enzo headed to his crib in West Bloomfield. The three-bedroom home was perfect for him. He could have honestly downsized, but he loved the spacious layout. As soon as he was inside, a text from Chasney came through.

I'm ready to go already. You still awake?

Yeah. I'm up. I'll turn my ringer on, so I can know when you outside.

Okay. I can't wait to taste you.

Enzo knew she had reached her limit when she started talking freaky. He shot her a wink emoji back and locked his phone after turning his volume up. Stripping from his clothes, Enzo let out a much-needed yawn and walked inside his bathroom, stark naked. Turning the shower on, he glanced at the security camera screen that was plastered on the wall in front of the toilet. It was detachable and could be placed anywhere in the bathroom. Though his neighborhood was considered one of the safest, he wasn't taking any chances with any of the muthafuckas around there. He'd pop their ass in a heartbeat if they felt the need to run down on him.

After showering, Enzo brushed his teeth, tossed on a pair of boxers, grabbed his remote and climbed in bed. It had been so long since he had been able to just chill, his entire body relaxed against the fresh sheets. Thanks to a cleaning service Grady had gotten him hip to, they had come through and cleaned his crib while he was away and just before he arrived.

Not realizing he had even fallen asleep, the ringing of his phone jarred him from his sleep. Knowing exactly who it was calling, he didn't bother to answer. Climbing from the bed, he trekked down the steps, and checked through the peephole before pulling it open for Chasney. Drunkenly, she waved bye to Dia and stepped inside.

"Did I wake you?" she asked in a giggle.

"Yeah. With your drunk ass. Come on. I'm tired as fuck."

Smacking her on the ass, Chasney walked ahead of him and up the steps. Enzo climbed in the bed and watched with low eyes as she stripped from her clothes and walked naked to the bathroom to shower. Ten minutes later, Chasney climbed into the bed, oiled down and horny as hell. Cuddling up next to Enzo, she ran her hand up his chest and placed kisses on his neck.

"Baby," she let out softly. "I missed you."

Finding his lips in the dark, Chasney kissed them before sucking the bottom one into her mouth. Moaning, she stuck her hand in the band of his boxers and massaged his growing member. Enzo laid there fully awake now, but not to the point where he wanted to put in work. In fact, he was contemplating even fucking Chasney. Thoughts of Harlem laid up in the bed they shared on many of nights invaded his mind. When Chasney climbed atop him and tried sliding onto him with no rubber, Enzo almost tossed her ass off the bed.

"You know better," he chastised. "Lift up so I can grab a rubber."

"Why?" she whined. "You can pull out."

Nixing her comment off, Enzo leaned over and grabbed a

condom from his nightstand. After securely sheathing himself, he slid into Chasney's gushy, tight walls.

"Shit," he hissed, forgetting how tight her shit was. Plus, it had been long overdue for her to take his large dick.

"Oh fuck."

Rolling her hips, Chasney tried to go slow so she could adjust to his girth, but Enzo wasn't having that. Thrusting his hips upward, he pushed the remainder of himself deep inside and bit his bottom lip.

"You climbed up here, you better ride this muthafucka."

Doing exactly what he said, Chasney leaned over and kissed his lips. This go around, Enzo tongued her down as her walls tightened with each stroke he delivered to her center. He knew this would be the last time he slid up inside of her, and he really wanted to give her lazy dick, but he didn't know what that was. Any female he slid inside of got at least grade C dick from him. Piping Chasney down with grade A at two in the morning wasn't happening though. She was getting an A- at best.

Rolling them over so he was on top, Enzo pushed her legs back and delivered deep strokes that had her head spinning. Missionary was Chasney's favorite. Enzo's large dick seemed to fit all the way inside of her and touch places no man had ever in her twenty-seven years of living reached.

"Oh my gosh," she squealed, stomach tightening due to her brewing orgasm.

"You 'bout to cum?"

She nodded, though he couldn't see. He didn't need to see. Enzo felt her walls tightening, and that was good enough. Ten strokes later, Chasney's back arched away from the bed, and her soft moans echoed throughout the room. Pounding into her quivering center, Enzo released his seeds into the condom shortly after. Breathing hard, he dropped his head and closed his eyes, wishing he had nutted inside Harlem. Thoughts of him impregnating her with their offspring for the second go around filled his mind. That thought alone had Enzo pulling himself out of Chasney and climbing from the bed to discard the condom.

Damn, I miss my shorty.

The next morning, Enzo was up bright and early ready to start his day. Dressed in black jeans, a white tee and a Detroit fitted on his head, he sat at the edge of his bed. Shaking Chasney's leg, she stirred in her sleep and rolled over to face him.

"Hmm?" she groaned.

"Wake up. I need to talk to you."

Stretching under his Egyptian sheets that felt like butter against her skin, she yawned before propping her head up on her elbow. Seeing the serious expression on his face, Chasney sat all the way up and pulled the covers over her exposed C-cup breasts.

"What's wrong? You look like you have a lot on your mind."

This scene would have felt like déjà vu had he and Chasney shared the connection he and Harlem did. Breaking things off with Harlem was the hardest shit he ever had to do in his life.

"I'm moving back to Kansas City," he said evenly.

She blinked a few times as if seeing had any correlation with her hearing. It did not. "Since when?"

"That's where I been at. You know that."

"Yeah, but you have a life here now. I mean, I guess I'm just confused as to why now all of a sudden," she replied softly.

When Enzo gave her a blank stare, unwanted tears pooled in her eyes. Deep down, she knew he wasn't up and moving for any reason. He either got a job there, or a woman he was seeking was there. Chasney would bet her last it was the latter of the two.

"It's another woman?"

"It's always been another woman, Chas."

Her breath got caught in her chest at his declaration. Enzo wasn't trying to be an asshole but beating around the bush with her wasn't how they operated. He had always kept their dealings on the up and up. Chasney was honestly taken aback.

"Another woman since when Enzo? You've been... we've been seeing each other for two years now. Make this make sense, please."

He scrubbed a hand down his head. Enzo wasn't in the business of giving explanations. He had never been good at them, but he knew she deserved that much. It wasn't her fault his first love crept back into his life like the thief in the night she was. Some shit was just inevitable.

After running down the simpler version of reconnecting with his family and Harlem, Chasney sat stumped. Her heart was falling into small pieces as she stared into his enticing, loving eyes. Enzo had been everything she literally prayed for, but he wasn't hers. She was just borrowing him for the time being.

"I-I don't know what to say. Where does that leave us?" she asked in a shaky tone.

Enzo would suggest them being friends, but that was like a slap in the face. "I don't know, Chas. A nigga ain't trying to hurt you, but I see I already have."

A tear slowly rolled down her beautiful, blemish-free face and Enzo reached to wipe it away. For the second time in his life, he was the cause for a woman's tears he truly cared for. He hated seeing her hurt, but he knew dragging her into the situation he and Harlem were in was not an option. Harlem wasn't the type to come second to anyone. Little did Enzo know, Harlem wasn't thinking about his ass. She had a moment the night before but was over it now. Enzo had every right to have a companion ducked off where he had been living, and so did she. He was breaking it off with her for both their sake but could have honestly kept Chasney on standby because Harlem wasn't about to just jump headfirst into a relationship with him.

Shaking her head, Chasney chuckled. "I knew all of this

was too good to be true. I mean, look at you. Of course, you have a first love tucked away waiting to rekindle that slow burning flame and say fuck what you built with me, huh? Dia warned me this would happen."

"She warned you? Fuck does that mean?" Enzo hissed.

"Just like I said. Fine, educated black brotha comes to a new state and seems perfect, but of course, he has a past. We all do. That was my fault for falling for you."

"You act like you was in this shit alone," he griped, grabbing her hand as she tossed the covers off her.

"Was I not?"

The two stared one another down, daring the other to speak what they knew was the truth. Physically, Enzo was hers. Mentally and emotionally, Harlem owned that. She had stamped her name on him far before he knew what the hell was going on. When Enzo didn't answer, she snatched her hand from his grasp.

"It's fine. I'll move on. Find another man to love me the way you said you lo-"

"I never told you I loved you, Chasney," he said, cutting her off.

Pausing from picking up her jeans from the ground, Chasney shook her head. Enzo was correct. Those three words had never fallen from his lips to her ears, but his actions sure felt like love. Sadly, she was mistaken.

"Well, it damn sure felt like love. Thanks for the mirage. You're one hell of an actor," she hissed.

"Aight. Watch who the fuck you talking to. I kept it gutta with you from day one. You knew exactly what you were getting into when you approached me in the club. Just because you painted it out to be what it's not, don't make me a bad person. I fuck with you heavy, but my heart ain't in this with you. You can't fault a nigga for being real. Ain't that what your ass told me you wanted from day one?"

Sniffling, Chasney ignored him and continued to get dressed in her attire from the night before. Every word Enzo was saying was one hundred percent accurate. She just hated that he was saying them right now. She didn't want him to be right. She didn't want to feel like a fool for loving him and for once, just wanted him to be wrong about something between them.

"Listen, Enzo," she breathed out after collecting her bearings. "I don't want us to end on bad terms. I get it. You're in love with someone else. I can't control that, but you can't sit here and tell me this doesn't feel like more than what you're not trying to express it is."

"It ain't. We're really good friends, Chas. On the real, you my nigga. We vibe and shit, but that's where it stops. I could see myself with you had I not already known who was meant for me. That's not to say you aren't meant for someone. That someone just isn't me, ma."

If she wanted the real, it didn't get any realer than that. Chasney was mature. She could handle lots of things thrown her way and had all her life, but this was really throwing her for a loop. *Had the signs always been there?* She had to question herself. Rather the signs were there or not; she had been too caught up in everything Enzo to catch onto them.

Nodding, Chasney exhaled a deep breath. "Okay, Enzo. So, what? You expect me to just move on?"

"Nah. I don't honestly, but I wasn't going to throw out the suggestion to be friends. I mean, unless you cool with that?"

"Is the girl you're in love with, your friend?"

"My best fucking friend. Our relationship is on a different level."

Chasney chuckled. "Well, there's no competing with that. Not like I would anyway, but I guess we can remain cordial. We did start off as friends first."

Enzo stood from the bed. "Exactly. It's up to you, though. I ain't pressuring you for no friendship, but I'd be lying if I said I'm not going to miss you."

Chasney closed her eyes to keep her tears at bay. "Do you have to leave?"

Pulling her into his chest, Enzo wiped away her tears and rubbed her back. He was such a fucking gentleman and asshole in one breath, that's why Chasney was confused. How the hell was he cutting off things between them and being so attentive as well? Not to mention the bomb dick he dropped off on her earlier that morning. *Whoever this woman is, is damn lucky.*

"I do."

"Can I at least come visit or you come here? What'd

Nello say about this move?" she asked, talking about Arie's brother he did business with.

Chasney knew they were close, but not to what extent. That was another reason Enzo knew she wasn't the woman for him. He hadn't opened up to her completely about what he really did for a living.

"Don't worry about Nello. We good."

She nodded. "Okay. Answer my question. You gone fly me out or come here? I'm holding you to this friendship thing."

"You know it ain't shit to fly you to me. That's what you want?"

When she nodded and poked out her lip, Harlem's words rang loudly in his ear. *And so is the bitch you down there pacifying.* He chuckled, thinking about her slick mouth. Enzo knew he'd face the consequences later on for agreeing to fly her out, but right now he just wanted to cheer her up. Pacify her feelings as Harlem stated.

"Yes. I'd love that *friend*," she grinned, making Enzo crack a smile.

"Aight. I got you. You got all your stuff? I'll drop you off at home before I make some moves."

Chasney scanned the carpeted area where her things were tossed last night, and nodded. "Can you at least buy me breakfast, damn? Break my heart then just send me home. I'll be better off taking an Uber," she said playfully.

"Shit. You can if you serious."

Smacking him in the chest, Chasney laughed. "I wish you would. You're going to feed me, then take me home," she said, wrapping her arms around his waist. Her head stopping at the center of his chest.

"In that order?"

"In that order."

Bending down, Enzo kissed her cheek. "Aight."

When they pulled away, and Chasney headed for the bathroom, Enzo let out a sigh of relief. He knew it'd be somewhat of a task ending things between them, but he didn't think it'd go over this smoothly. He was appreciative of Chasney being mature about the situation for real. She could have spazzed, and he'd see why. Two years is a lot of investing, especially emotionally. The reason Enzo could let go so easily was because he wasn't as invested as she was. And, that right there could have been a cause for disaster had he not been who he was; Enzo muthafuckin' Maverick.

CHAPTER FIVE

"You know what you want?" Harlem asked Bree.

Wanting to spend some time with her family, Harlem decided to take them out to dinner at *Texas Roadhouse*. Andrea didn't feel like cooking and neither did she. Staring at her little sister, Harlem couldn't help but grin at how much she had grown.

"I want a steak," Bree replied.

"A steak?" Harlem questioned.

Andrea just snickered. She knew her baby girl could eat.

Innocently, Bree shot Harlem a grin. "Yes. With a loaded baked potato, shrimp and a salad."

"Bruh, you greedy," Davion said, looking up from his phone.

His head had been buried in his phone the entire ride to the restaurant and in it since they'd sat down.

"You eat more than me," Bree shot back.

"I ain't ordering no steak though. That's for grown people."

"Mama," Bree whined.

Andrea shook her head. "Will you two stop? Get whatever you want, Bree. And, you," she hissed Davion's way. "Put your phone up while we're spending quality time together."

"You don't pay my phone bill."

"Excuse me?" Andrea hissed at the same time as Harlem spoke.

"Who the hell are you talking to like that?" she spat, snatching his phone out of his hand. "You ain't grown. It don't matter who pay this bill; do what she said."

Davion mumbled something under his breath and Harlem almost reached across the table to snatch him up. She had no clue where his disrespectful behavior had surfaced from, but he had better get himself together and quick.

"What was said?" Harlem hissed.

"Nothing."

"Good. You can kiss this phone, your ass doesn't pay the bill for goodbye, since you wanna talk about someone paying the bill for something. I don't know what's gotten into you, but you better find some manners and quick."

Davion was so mad, his nose flared as he mugged Harlem. He could be mad all he wanted to be, but Harlem didn't care. Regardless of the type of mother Andrea had been to them in the last five years, disrespecting her wasn't about to fly.

"Sorry, mama," Davion grumbled lowly.

"Sorry for what?" Harlem spat.

Davion clenched his teeth together. "Sorry for disrespecting you."

The only thing Andrea could do was nod her head. Harlem had stepped in and checked his ass so quickly; she didn't even have time to react. Sliding his phone into her purse, Harlem snatched the drink menu up. She needed an alcoholic beverage pronto. The water they started her off with wasn't going to do.

"Can I still get a steak?" Bree whispered, making Harlem crack a smile even though she was hot.

"Go ahead, Bree."

"Yes," she cheered, tossing her fist into the air.

The waitress came through and took their orders. Harlem was always amazed at how grown her siblings had gotten and hearing them recite their orders, when just years prior they couldn't pronounce certain words, had her grinning. She was a proud big sister and vowed that if she ever had to go through what she had gone through again just to see them progress in life, she would.

"I'ma go use the restroom before they bring our drinks out," Andrea announced.

Harlem replied an okay and kept looking over the menu. She was undecided between a steak as well or the salmon.

Having not eaten anything all day but an omelet that morning, she'd more than likely order both. As soon as Andrea was out of earshot, Harlem called Davion's name to grab his attention. Placing his menu down, he looked her in the eyes.

"I know mama has had some rough days, but there's no need for you to be disrespecting her."

"She doesn't pay the bill, though."

Harlem sighed. That wasn't the point she was trying to get across. "We know that. Does that give you a right to just talk to her how you did? Do you always talk to her like that?"

Davion sucked his teeth. "Nah. I mean, not all the time, but she be making me mad. We all know the only thing she pays for is those pills she be swallowing. Everything else we always need comes from your pockets. I just miss the old her."

Harlem's throat ached at his admission. Honestly, she missed the old Andrea as well. Before the abuse. Before the depression. Before the pill-popping days. She was trying though, and Davion didn't see that. He never wanted to be that son to disrespect his mama, and he hadn't been, but he was going through his teenage stages of life without a positive example of a male around.

Though Chazz had been released from jail two years prior, the relationship with his kids wasn't the same, and he knew it wouldn't be. So many years had separated their growth, and he was stuck trying to play catch up, but it was too late. They had practically raised themselves.

"We all do, but just know she's trying, okay? You talking

to her like that is not cool and only going to make her sadder. You're the man of the house, right?" Harlem asked, trying to lighten the mood back up.

"Yes," he answered confidently.

"Well act like it. Men do not disrespect their mothers, let alone get their phones taken by their big sister."

He shot her a handsome grin. "Aight. I'm sorry, sis."

"Mhm. I know you are. You aren't off the hook that easily, though."

He wasn't getting that phone back until they were done eating. Harlem loved her siblings dearly, damn near more than she loved herself and would give them her last. The last thing she wanted either of them doing was coming down hard on Andrea. Unbeknownst to Harlem, Andrea hadn't had any pills for a week. That was the longest she had gone without popping one. Had she thought about it? Yes, but she was trying to wing herself off them. As Harlem picked her sides for both entrees she was going to order, Andrea came back to the booth and had company with her.

"Well, hello niece."

Looking up at where the voice came from, Harlem's skin grew warmer at the person before her. She glanced in Andrea's direction and she looked beyond annoyed.

"Auntie," Bree squealed, hopping up from her seat.

As Bree wrapped her arms around Kishana, Dre's sister, she wore a smirk on her face that made Harlem's skin crawl. Walking up behind her was Dre's mama, Rochelle. Harlem couldn't stand her messy ass, and she knew for a fact some shit was about to go down.

"Look at the happy family out enjoying themselves," Rochelle said with a smirk identical to her daughter's.

"Hi, Granny," Bree spoke, giving her a hug before sitting down.

"Can we help you with something?" Harlem asked as calmly as possible.

"As a matter of fact, you could. So you see, we ran into Ms. Andrea here in the restroom, and she seemed to have left something behind," Kishana said, waving the baggie of pills in the air.

Harlem's eyes shot over to her mama's at the same time Davion's did. Andrea's mouth went dry. She hadn't popped a pill while in the restroom, but she sure had thought about it. Inside the stall, she had taken the baggie out, stared at it, and shook her head before stuffing it back into her pants pocket. When she went to pee and pulled her pants down, the baggie fell out of her pocket, but she didn't hear it. There were only about five pills in the bag.

When she was at the sink washing her hands, Kishana came out of the stall next to her after picking up the baggie. She was ready to hand the woman her pills back but realized who she was and pocketed them instead. They shared a few brief words before Kishana walked out and back to their table to get her mama. When Andrea did finally walk out of the restroom, they were right behind her.

Davion shook his head and groaned, "See." Everything he had just said was considered facts in his eyes.

"You need to give me my shit back," Andrea spat, trying to snatch the baggie out of Kishana's hand but she moved it out of arms reach. Parties in earshot of their table turned their head in their direction.

"Or what? You gone have me set up like you did my brother?" Kishana hissed.

"Kishana. Let's not go there in these people's restaurant. Just give her the baggie back."

"Nah. She ain't getting a damn thing back until she confesses to us and to Bree how she had someone kill Dre. We deserve the truth," Rochelle yelled.

Bree's curious, confused eyes danced between her daddy's people, and Harlem. Her brain was trying to process what was going on, and she hated how her little heart began to feel inside. Seeing the look on her sister's face, Harlem stood to her feet.

"Listen. This is not the time nor place for y'all to be doing all this. Your son has been gone for years now, and you're still looking for someone to blame. Blame yourself."

"Bitch. You got us fucked up," Kishana spat, pushing Harlem into the table.

Not giving her a chance to process what she had just done, Harlem picked up the glass of water so quick and smashed it into her face, Kishana didn't see what hit her. She felt it though. Tossing the glass to the side, Harlem delivered vicious blows to the girl's face and sent body shots that had her buckling at the knees. Davion, Bree and Andrea were screaming her name, but she was so zoned out in the ass whooping she was giving, she didn't hear them until a male customer from a nearby table was swooping her up.

"Whoa, ma. Chill, chill," he demanded, holding her tightly in a bear hug.

Staring down at Kishana's bloody, battered face, the only thing Harlem could do was lick her lips and breath hard.

"Look what you did to her face!" Rochelle screamed, hysterically trying to get to Harlem, but Andrea pushed her back so hard, she went tumbling to the ground right next to her daughter.

"Ladies, we're gonna have to ask you guys to leave or the police will be called," the manager stated.

"They came over here starting with us!" Davion hissed, grilling the male manager upside his head. He was ready to get a round in too, with whoever. Seeing his big sister throw hands like that had him hype.

"Let me go," Harlem told the guy who was holding her. His grip was strong as hell, and now that she had come back to her senses, he smelled damn good too.

"You sure you ain't gone run up on her?"

"Positive. Now, let me go."

Doing as he was told, he unclasped his arms from around Harlem, but didn't move an inch just in case she felt froggy and decided to leap. Kishana was so fucked up, both eyes were damn near shut closed, and her face was swelling.

"Not you guys," the manager said. "Them."

When he pointed to Kishana and Rochelle, Harlem smirked.

"She just attacked us, and you're throwing us out? You'll be hearing from my lawyer," Rochelle hissed, standing to her feet.

Helping Kishana up, blood leaked onto the tile floor profusely. One of the employees snatched up a handful of napkins and handed them to her, as another one hustled away to get the mop. As the manager walked them toward the front door, Harlem finally glanced over at Bree and her heart sank to the pit of her stomach. She had tears in her eyes and they were filled with confusion.

The guy who snatched Harlem up returned to his table as they returned to theirs. Sitting down next to Bree, Harlem looked at her and released a deep sigh.

"I'm sorry y'all had to see me wild out like that," she apologized.

"It's cool, sis. You gave ole girl the hands," Davion encouraged with a wide grin spread across his face. His adrenaline was pumping.

"They were out of line for that," Andrea spoke up and said.

"Were they?"

Harlem shot the question Andrea's way and kept her

pensive gaze on her until Andrea looked away. She wanted to say much more, but she knew it wasn't the time.

"Absolutely. You can test me right now since you have that look on your face. I already know what you're thinking."

"Are you all doing okay? Can I get you anything besides the food that's almost ready?" their waitress asked, putting a halt to their conversation.

Harlem looked around the table and saw the only thing missing was her glass of water. "Sure. Another water and a Sangria Margarita on the rocks with an extra Patron shot."

"Ooh. Can I have one?" Davion belted out.

"You have some i.d., man?" The waitress laughed, knowing he wasn't old enough.

"Don't pay him any mind. Oh, and some fresh rolls and that's all."

The waitress nodded and let them know she'd be right back. The table got eerily quiet for a minute or so before the silence was broken by Bree.

"What she said about my daddy... is it true?" she said in almost a whisper like tone.

Harlem's eyes shot upward to her mama's, and she couldn't read the expression on her mother's face. Knowing that what had just gone down was heavy on Bree's mind, Harlem quickly tried to think of an answer that would suffice but couldn't. Bree was inquisitive. Harlem could have simply said no, and Bree would have turned around and asked 'Well, why did she say that?' and Harlem knew why but would never tell. That was one secret she was going to take to her grave.

"No, Bree. It's not true," Harlem replied.

"Well, why did she-"

"Who had the steak?" A waiter asked, as they began bringing their food out.

Saved by the food, Harlem thought, thankful as ever for a distraction. As Bree examined her plate, she looked up at her big sister and the worry on her face. Nudging her arm, Harlem glanced her way.

"What's wrong?" Harlem asked. "You don't want the steak?"

"It's good. I was just going to say thank you for bringing us out to eat."

Harlem's heart swelled. "Of course, boo. You know I'd do anything for y'all."

"Anything?" Bree asked with questioning eyes.

It was as if she was staring directly into Harlem's soul the stare was so intense. Without batting an eye, Harlem nodded her head.

"Anything is this world."

Bree smiled, and Harlem relaxed some. Only some because she knew there'd be more questions where the ones from tonight had come from and there'd be no distractions then. Harlem only hoped and prayed the other parts of her past stayed where they were at and didn't resurface. Explaining to her sister how Enzo killed her daddy was not something she ever planned to mark on her calendar. She just had to take it to her grave if the universe allowed her to do so.

Laid out on her sectional couch, Yaz had her phone to her ear listening to Harlem tell her about everything that went down a few nights ago when they were out to eat.

"That bitch was out of line," she said, rolling her eyes.

"And, what's even crazier is I don't know what happened to those damn pills."

"Now you know one of those employees snatched those up," Yaz laughed. "Andrea wasn't getting those back."

Harlem snickered and got serious. "I'm just pissed I had to do all that in front of them. Had I gone to jail over that shit, I would have really been pissed."

Thanks to a few witnesses, when the police did arrive, nothing happened. Harlem told her side of the story and the employees backed her up as well as a few other parties who witnessed the altercation. In fact, their section clapped because Harlem was in no way wrong for beating Kishana's ass. She had the balls and energy to push her; she should have kept that same energy when it was time to throw hands.

"I would have bailed you out. What Enzo say about his little Laila Ali?" Yaz laughed.

"Girl. I'm not thinking about no damn Enzo. His ugly ass went out of town a week ago and ain't back yet."

"He got a chick up there, right?"

"Mhm. He claims he's handling business though, so whatever. That ain't my nigga," Harlem huffed.

"Whatever. You know if he popped up at your crib right now, you'd be busting that pussy open for him."

Harlem smirked. She sure would, but that wasn't any of Yaz' business. "Nah. I'm putting his ass on punishment and getting me a new nigga."

"What's up with you and Kartel?"

She rolled her eyes at the mention of his name. "Not a damn thing. He brought me some food the other week and ate my pussy, but that's it. He been on the blocklist since."

Yaz shook her head. She thought she was coldhearted and mean to niggas; Harlem was vicious with it.

"I don't know why he puts up with your ass."

"I don't either. I would have been stopped fucking with me," Harlem laughed. "You're one to talk. You cheating on Nova, so let's not get on me."

"No, I am not."

"Yeah, not anymore. You being faithful now?" she snickered.

A text came through on Yaz' line, and she pulled the phone from her ear and placed it on speaker while turning the volume down.

"I had one slip up and now I'm a cheater," she said dryly as her eyes went wide at the text she just received from Lucci.

Come outside.

"What the hell?" Yaz whispered, hopping up from the couch.

"What?"

Peeking out of her curtains, Yaz' jaw dropped. Parked backwards in her driveway was Lucci's white, heavily tinted Audi Truck.

"Bitch. Why did this nigga Lucci just text me and say come outside?" she whispered in a hiss.

"Um," Harlem laughed. "Because he wants to see you? Is he out there?"

"Yes, and Nova is upstairs sleeping. What the fuck!"

"Oh. He's bold," Harlem chuckled. "What you gon' do?"

"Tell him to take his ass home. I don't know why he thought poppin' up over here was cool. He tripping, tripping." Typing out a reply on her phone, Yaz sent him a message back.

No. Take your ass home.

Nah. Bring your ass here or I'm coming the fuck in. Ringing the doorbell and all.

Groaning, Yaz sent him a bunch of middle finger emoji's. "He is on some bullshit."

"What you gon' do?" Harlem squealed. "You know he ain't wrapped too tight. That nigga will mess around and honk his horn."

Beep! Beep!

The sentence hadn't even left Harlem's mouth completely and Lucci was outside blowing his horn. Yaz jumped and hurriedly rushed to the front door where her Gucci slides were.

"I'ma smack the fuck out of this nigga!" Yaz hissed as Harlem laughed so hard she had tears in her eyes.

"I know his ass didn't just honk!?"

"Yes. I shoulda never fucked this stupid ass nigga."

"You live, and you learn, boo. Call me later and tell me what happens."

Yaz told her she would and released a deep breath. Fucking around with Lucci was going to get her into some shit she couldn't get out of, but she'd be lying if she said she didn't like the crazy feeling that had come over her. Opening the door, she was greeted with the cool breeze of the nighttime air. Shutting it as silently as she could, Yaz walked down the few steps and padded down the concrete driveway with an attitude. Peeping her in the side mirror, Lucci hit his locks and she eased inside. She wanted to slam his door so fucking hard, just to piss him off but she shut it like she had some sense.

"What the fuck is wrong with you?" she grilled him, not bothering to speak.

The potent smell of weed was floating through the air. Lucci licked his plump lips and smirked. "What's wrong with me? You the one got a muthafuckin' attitude. Whaddup?"

"Yes, I have an attitude. You can't just be poppin' up at my house like this. My man is inside."

Lucci's brow lifted. "Word?"

He acted like he was about to climb out and Yaz tugged on his arm. "Quit playing all the time. What do you want and make this quick?"

"Why you been ignoring my texts?"

"You drove all the way over here to ask about some text messages?" she chuckled.

"What it look like? You been ignoring me ever since you slid through the house a few weeks ago. What I do to you?"

"Nothing. I just had to remind myself that I'm in a relationship, that's all. What you tripping for?"

Lucci sucked his teeth. "Man, ain't nobody tripping."

"Popping up at another nigga's woman's crib at ten at night is definitely considered tripping," Yaz laughed. "It's okay. I get it. You missed me. If I was you, I'd miss me too."

"Nah. I missed that wet pussy you got between your legs. I ain't miss your ass."

Yaz busted out laughing. "Whatever, nigga. You don't have to admit it to me. Your actions tell me everything I need to know."

"Yeah, aight. What you was in there doing? Got these lil' ass shorts on," he said, slapping her exposed thigh, before caressing it.

Yaz pushed his hand away. "Talking to Harlem."

"I can touch you, girl," he chuckled, moving his hand up her thigh.

Yaz' heart rate increased as he slowly caressed her pussy through her shorts. She tried moving his hand away by grabbing his wrist, but that didn't help. Leaning over the console, Lucci placed soft kisses against her neck. The truth was he did miss her reckless ass and he hated that she had went missing on him. Had she replied to his messages, Lucci wouldn't have resorted to poppin' up on her but he had to do what he had to do. Yaz needed to understand that what Lucci wanted, Lucci got; that included her.

"Lucc, stop," Yaz groaned, moving her head away from him.

"C'mere," he demanded saucily, snatching her out of her seat in one breath. Those years in jail had paid off for sure. He lifted Yaz' thick ass up with ease and sat her on his lap.

"No. No. We are not about to do this," Yaz said, fighting to get out of his grasp.

Smacking her on her ass cheek that was now exposed, Lucci hissed, "Yes, we are."

Kissing on her hardened nipples in the tank top she was wearing, Lucci massaged her ass, making her grind on his dick. He was hardening underneath the softness of her plump booty and Yaz' pussy was betraying her in every way as she felt it contract.

"You gone stop ignoring me," he said, pulling her hair in the ponytail it was in.

"Ouch, nigga!"

"Shut up. You sneaking your ass out the house to see me, you about to ride this dick."

Slipping his hand in the leg hole of her shorts, Lucci slipped two fingers inside her with ease. Yaz was so wet, the sounds of her juices sounded off throughout the truck.

"Oh my gosh. This is so wrong," she whined, rotating her hips.

"Nah. This just right. This pussy wet as hell, too."

Pulling his fingers out of her, Lucci slipped his hand in the shorts he was wearing and rubbed her juices over his dick before freeing it. Yaz shook her head at him not wearing any boxers or briefs.

"You just knew you were sliding up in this, huh?"

"I'm always sure. Lift up."

Doing as she was told, Lucci grabbed a condom and slid it on. Playing around in her wetness, Lucci smacked her ass and pulled her down onto his throbbing dick.

"Ssss," Yaz hissed.

Caught up in the feel of her tight, wet walls on his dick, Lucci pulled Yaz to him and kissed her lips. When he realized he had just kissed her for the first time, he didn't even pull away. Instead, he stuck his tongue in her mouth and adjusted his seat, so he was leaning back. Clapping her ass cheeks, Yaz rode him with fervor. The idea of getting caught or seen by any of her neighbors or Nova only heightened her arousal. Roughly, Lucci gripped both of her chocolate ass cheeks in his hands.

"Why this pussy so tight? Huh?"

Yaz wasn't about to answer him. The dick he was plunging was damn near reaching her chest. Smirking, Lucci made circles on her clit with his thumb that had her bucking at the hips.

"Oooh, shit. Wait," she purred, throwing her head back. "This is so wrong."

"That nigga can't be fucking you right. This shit don't make no sense," Lucci grumbled as she grinded harder on his steel.

Leaning forward, Yaz rose up some and slammed her pussy up and down on him repeatedly. If she was going to fuck him and risk her relationship for the hundredth time, she might as well have gotten a good nut off. The way she was bouncing all over him had Lucci ready to take her ass in the house and fuck the dog shit out of her. Yaz felt like she was in control as she rode his dick like a pro.

"Look at you. Showing out on this dick. Ride this muthafucka just like that," he groaned, pinching her nipples.

Arching her back more, Yaz felt her orgasm so close, she squeezed her eyes shut. Deep down, she felt so bad for fucking Lucci right outside of her house while Nova was sleeping, but in her mind, she didn't have a choice. Lucci had claimed he was just giving her dick, but the truth was he had caught feelings for Yaz long before he sampled her pussy. The letters and phone calls they shared while he was locked down was more than just passing some time by. Though Yaz wasn't showing signs of loyalty right now, with her fucking another man while in a relationship, Lucci summed it up as her loyalty belonging to him and she was in a relationship just because.

Damn. Do I got feelings for another's nigga bitch?

When he felt Yaz' legs tremble and muscles tighten, Lucci shook his head and pulled her to him by the back of her neck. He most definitely had some type of feelings for Yaz and didn't know how to feel about that shit. The stunts she was pulling was some straight freaky hoe shit, but Lucci loved it. Sadly, he loved a female that did what the fuck she wanted to do. That was until she got with him.

Lucci didn't have any intentions on taking Yaz from her nigga, but she wasn't making it hard for him not to either. If he knew what was best for him though, Lucci had better take heed. Yaz was the type of bitch niggas would grow to hate because she gave no fuck about their feelings. They were playing a dangerous game, and there could only be one winner when this was all over and done with.

CHAPTER SIX

"You're letting me go?" Zeema asked lowly, surprise laced through her words.

Harlem stood in front of her with a pair of scissors in her hand, ready to cut the tight ass rope Vonzell had her tied up in. After weeks of doing drop-ins and checking on her, Harlem was tired of it all. Shit on the streets had died down behind Trill and his crews' murders, and in her eyes, if Zeema did decide to snitch after all this time, she was either going to get popped by those wanting to retaliate or go to jail as an accessory. The choice would be hers. She had a baby to worry about, so Harlem hopped she made the right decision.

Her family had put up missing person flyers and posts, but she was very much alive. As unfortunate as it had been to be held hostage, Zeema learned to not ever fuck with Harlem again. The only reason she didn't kill her was because of the baby she was carrying.

"Yeah. Sick of coming here. Just know from here on out, you are dead to me. Stay clear from me, where I be at, the people I fuck with and especially away from Enzo. I spared your life, but my nigga will kill you. Period."

Chills shot through Zeema's entire body as she nodded. "Okay. I-I got it."

"Good. Now, I'ma untie this rope. You try any slick shit like you did with my boy and I'ma do much worse than punch you. Got it?"

She nodded her head vehemently. "Y-Yes. I swear I won't try anything."

Pulling her gun from her waist just in case, Harlem took it off safety and walked over to her. Bending down, she cut the rope around her ankles first before cutting the ones on her wrists. Zeema's body was so sore; she couldn't put up a fight if she wanted to. Sitting in a chair for twenty-four hours a day was beyond horrible. She was sure she had gotten butt sores and some more shit while being tied down.

Rubbing her aching wrists, she looked up at Harlem. "Thank you. I'm so sorry for not being a good friend to you. You didn't do anything but look out for me, and I crossed you."

"I'm not trying to hear that emotional, fake bullshit honestly. You knew what the fuck you were doing way before you fucked Trill. Way before you told that friend of yours my business, and way before you pulled that shit at Briscoe's crib. Don't thank me. Thank God. If I had my way, I'd slice your fucking neck and have the pit bulls in the backyard play fetch with your head."

Zeema swallowed hard as tears gathered in her eyes. She was not expecting Harlem to say that at all. Vonzell had brought the pits in a few times during her stay and they growled at her the entire time. They knew people only got brought to the house if they were about to lose their life.

"Just so I'm clear; I do not fuck with you anymore. Count your days and blessings, because karma is real, and she attacks bitches like you, chews you up and swallows. Just be grateful you have a little time before she makes her appearance."

When Harlem smiled, Zeema knew she had fucked with a real-life psycho. When Vonzell walked in from one of the back rooms, he frowned at Zeema being untied and mugged Harlem.

"It was fun, right?" he asked Zeema, who didn't bother to give him a reply.

"Call up one of your drivers and have them take her to where she needs to go," Harlem instructed him.

She was done with this chapter of her life, at least for now. Harlem wasn't worried about her snitching. Zeema would be a fool to do such a stupid thing, especially while she was pregnant. She wasn't going to take Harlem's promises lightly either. They weren't threats at this point, because she was sure if Enzo saw her out, he'd really have her body missing never to be found ever.

After one of Vonzell's boys showed up, who Harlem gave a good pay for his services to, Zeema was escorted to the back of the car with a blindfold around her eyes. Vonzell climbed in the seat next to her and they pulled off. She no longer had a car, and her house had been searched by her family, so she honestly didn't know where to go. The only person she could think of was Ranisha, so that's where she told them to head to. After being presumed missing for weeks, Zeema popping back up with a round belly at that was about to look suspicious as hell, but she was determined to make up a lie and a damn good one. Traumatized by the entire ordeal or not, she valued her and her unborn child's life more than anything right now.

When Harlem made it home, she showered, tossed on one of Enzo's tank tops and climbed in bed. She wasn't tired, but it felt good to just relax. Scrolling through her Pinterest app for new furniture for her living room ideas, she somehow stumbled upon a sexy hand-drawn photo of a male and a female with masks on. The male was shirtless with tattoos covering his body, while the female stood behind him with a pointed gun. She smiled and saved the picture before switching apps.

Going to her Instagram page, she uploaded the picture, making it black and white. The caption read *#HoodLove*.

It reminded her of her and Enzo so much, she started to send it to him too, but remembered she wasn't fucking with him at the moment. Continuing to scroll Instagram, Harlem came across a flyer for a Labor Day barbecue the following week that Briscoe was throwing. She couldn't believe how quickly the summer was flying by, but she wasn't complaining. She didn't hate the summer but loved the winter. That's when she could really pull out her threads. Taking a screenshot of the flyer, she sent it to Yaz and Dreka in their group chat.

All the drug dealers are going to be out, bitch! – Yaz
Like you need another one, hoe. – Dreka
I just want some food. Fuck them niggas lol. – Harlem

Harlem could already taste the grilled hotdog and ribs. Briscoe could throw down on the grill and she couldn't wait. There were going to be plenty of caked up niggas out that day, but she wasn't trying to talk to anyone new. Not yet, at least. She wasn't necessarily waiting around for Enzo either. Him being away in Detroit and tending to his business told Harlem everything she needed to know. They weren't ready for anything serious with one another.

She was fine with that, though. For so long, Harlem hadn't even dated, let alone been interested in a nigga unless she was running in his pockets. Maybe this time around, since Enzo popped back into her life, she'd try to take the male species serious.

"We'll see how that goes," she chuckled before texting her friends back.

Sometimes I can't sleep, waking up in cold sweats
Nightmares of a torturous and bloody slow death
I jump up and grab my heat, aim it 'round the room
Somebody tryna get on me, mind playin' tricks on me

The music blasting from the speaker nearby had Harlem bobbing her head and rapping along with Young Devi as Briscoe placed three ribs on her plate. She already had a hot dog, baked beans, and macaroni and cheese on another.

"You rapping like this yo' shit," he joked.

"It is," she chuckled, biting into her hot dog. "Can you hide me one of these for later?"

"Yeah, I got you, fatty."

Harlem slapped his arm. "I am not fat. You the one with the dad belly now," she teased.

Briscoe had put on a few pounds since his daughter was born, but he didn't care. He called it happy weight, though his baby mama, Raniya was far from happy. She had caught wind of him fucking Ranisha, her sister, and all hell had broken loose. Though he hadn't fucked her in months, the damage was already done. Their sisterly bond would never be the same.

Rubbing his hand over his stomach, Briscoe grinned, "The ladies still love me."

"I bet they do."

Harlem's eyes roamed the park that was packed with people of all ages. In her mind, Labor Day wasn't a reserved holiday she really cared to go all out for. Not the way some black folks did. She was positive almost everyone was just happy to be off from work and to eat some barbeque. Harlem most certainly was. Making her way to the table she, Yaz, Dreka, and Mina, Dreka's cousin had snagged, she sat down with a huff.

"What's wrong with you?" Yaz questioned.

"Out of breath, hell," Harlem huffed, grabbing her Styrofoam cup that was filled with D'ussé and cran-apple juice. There was hardly any juice thanks to Yaz. Her heavy-handed ass was trying to get them turned up.

"I didn't think this many people would be here," Dreka said, scanning the park.

"Now you know Briscoe and his folks bring the people out," Yaz added. "Plus it's free food?"

"Exactly," Mina laughed. "No one is turning down free food."

"Well, hopefully, it stays peaceful. You know how niggas get," Harlem said, scooping up a spoonful of baked beans.

"And these females."

Harlem nodded and continued to bash her plate. She hadn't eaten all day just so she could save room for all the food she was about to indulge in. When she was halfway finished, she realized she hadn't seen Enzo not once since they arrived. She wasn't checking for him or anything; okay maybe she was, but she just found it strange that he hadn't returned from Detroit yet. If he had, she was clueless of his whereabouts.

"Look at your boo," Dreka smirked, nudging Yaz' arm.

Yaz rolled her eyes already knowing who she was speaking on. Posted up in the middle of the street where tons of cars were aligning the curb, Lucci was leaning shirtless on a money green Porsche truck. People were parked all in the grass because there was nowhere else to park on the street. A game of basketball was being held on the court. Kids were running around the play area without a care in the world, and Lucci was monitoring it all.

He knew for a fact some niggas would be on some funny shit with the majority of his crew in one place, so he was prepared for whatever. The extendo tucked in the band of his shorts was ready too.

"That is not my boo. I can't stand his ass," Yaz grumbled.

"Is that why you keep sitting on his dick?" Dreka questioned with a confused, playful expression on her face.

Yaz flicked her off and tossed the rest of her drink back. "Somehow, I keep falling on it. Whoops."

They all laughed, but Harlem's was cut short when she saw a black Maserati pull up to where Lucci and his boys were standing. She didn't realize until they had moved out of the way that they had been saving Enzo a parking spot. Harlem felt herself getting upset, but quickly checked herself. Grabbing her cup, she gulped it down in a few chugs and clenched her teeth.

"That look on your face can only mean one thing," Yaz said before looking to where Harlem's eyes were trained.

Stepping out of the car, Enzo smoothly adjusted his shirt. He was on his chill shit today, rocking a white *Champion* tee, black track pants that hung slightly from his waist, and a fresh pair of Forces. No matter how many tennis shoes came out, Forces were his favorite. When the passenger door opened,

Harlem frowned so hard she'd surely have wrinkles in her forehead by the day's end.

Rising from the passenger seat, Chasney closed the door behind her and fixed the strap on her purse that was sitting on her shoulder. Enzo had told her to leave it in the car, but she wasn't about to do that. She didn't care who he was.

"Oh shit," Yaz whispered just loud enough for only their table to hear her. "Who is that?"

Harlem had a clue of who the girl could be, but she didn't know her name nor did she want to. She now knew why Enzo had been ducked off for so long in Detroit and it had her hotter than a car that'd been sitting in one hundred degree plus temperature all day.

"Did he know you were going to be here?" Dreka asked her.

"It don't matter. We're not together."

Yaz waved her off dismissively. "Whatever. All that shit is irrelevant when he brings another bitch around. Let you have pulled up with another nigga then what?"

"Then nothing. I'm not tripping, for real. Enzo and I both know what it is. I knew about her," Harlem answered, hoping they'd drop the subject.

"Hmph. I guess. If that's what you say, then cool. Now, if something pops off, just give me a signal."

Harlem chuckled. "I'm chilling. Pour me another cup."

"You know how you get off that brown liquor," Dreka chimed. "Don't start showing your ass."

Smirking, Harlem just nodded her head as she watched Enzo slap hands with his boys. She saw Lucci nod his head in their direction and when Enzo was facing her, she gave him a wave.

"Boy, they shooting daggers like a muthafucka this way," Lucci laughed.

"I ain't worried. She knows what's up."

"Yeah… we gon' see. Who you?" Lucci asked, eyeing Chasney.

He knew who she was, but he just had to fuck with her for a little bit. Smiling, Chasney introduced herself.

"I'm Chasney and you are?"

"The nigga you probably won't ever see again," he laughed, and Chasney said 'oh,' surprised by his answer. "I'm fuckin' with you. I'm Lucci. Enzo's cousin."

"Nice to meet you. Can we get some food? I'm starving."

Her question was for Enzo, but Lucci answered her. Pointing to where the food was at, her stomach growled a little and Enzo chuckled. He had just picked her up from the airport after she had a layover and would've stopped to get something to eat, but they were headed straight to where all the food was. Though Enzo had lots of money, he was still tight with it.

"I'ma go get some food. Quit posting up like you ready for some shit to go down. Just chill," Enzo whispered in Lucci's ear.

"Nigga. I am chilling. Chilling and watching my surroundings. Go fix your girl a plate," he smirked.

"I'm not his girl," Chasney spoke up and said.

Lucci tossed his hands in the air and chuckled. "Ah shit. Well, excuse me. Let me mind my business, cuz."

"Yeah. You do that. Come on," Enzo said, lightly pushing Chasney forward.

Her eyes scanned the park until she located where the food was at. Harlem and her girls looked on as she climbed up the small grassy hill. Chasney wasn't necessarily barbeque attire ready, but she was dressed cute nonetheless. She and Enzo were almost dressed alike. The Nike fit she was wearing was made up of leggings, a tank top, and Air Maxes.

As they got closer, Harlem's eyes left Chasney's and landed on Enzo's. She was waiting to see if he was going to walk right by her or stop and speak. When she saw the grin on his face just a few steps away, she rolled her eyes.

"You can go get you a plate. I'ma holla at them real quick," Enzo told Chasney.

Her eyes did a quick sweep of the table trying to assess which one was the female who had Enzo's attention all of a sudden. Yaz was staring directly at her, so she chalked that up as it not being her. When she got to Harlem, her cheeks lifted approvingly and enviously. She wasn't jealous at all, but she could definitely see why Enzo was in love. The way Harlem was glaring at him, she almost felt bad, but not that bad.

"Okay," she said before walking off towards where Briscoe was at the grill.

Enzo watched her for a few seconds before his eyes dropped to where Harlem was sitting. Licking his lips, he leaned forward and placed a kiss on her cheek before whispering in her ear.

"Fix your face," he hissed lowly.

Harlem just rolled her eyes. "Whatever. Get out my face, Enzo."

Enzo brushed a hand over his fresh cut and chuckled. "So you gon' sit here and act like you don't miss me?"

Picking her refilled cup up, Harlem went to drink from it, but it was snatched out of her hand. Placing the cup to his lips, Enzo drunk damn near the entire drink before handing it back to her.

"So disrespectful," Yaz snickered, mimicking Big Boi from the movie *ATL*.

"What up, y'all," Enzo spoke before focusing his attention back on Harlem, who was still frowning.

The liquor in her system had her ready to punch him, but she kept reminding herself to chill out. Eyeing her fresh braids that took way too long to install, Enzo gripped the ponytail they were in and jerked her head back some.

"Stop," Harlem whined, pushing him.

"Nah. The fuck you got an attitude with me for?"

She slapped his hand away. "Because, nigga. Don't play

dumb. You said you were handling business. That don't look like business to me."

"That ain't even something you need to be worried about."

"Oh," Harlem chirped. "I ain't worried bout' nothing. Nigga, I ain't worried 'bout nothing. Nigga, I ain't worried 'bout nothing," she sang as Yaz adlibbed.

"Haaan," Yaz belted, sounding like French Montana.

Their table cracked up laughing and Enzo just shook his head. The empty bottle on the table let him know they were about to be with the shits all evening. Knowing how reckless Harlem and her girls were, Enzo was starting to regret flying Chasney out. He hadn't been in Detroit like Harlem assumed, but right in the city making business moves.

For three days straight, he and Deuce sat and hacked into any systems or programs Enzo may have used while scamming. Though Nello had assured him he was good to go; he still had Deuce run his scan through everything. He could never be too safe. It'd be just his luck to try and get out the scamming world only to get jammed up because he failed to cover his tracks thoroughly. He'd be sick as fuck if that happened.

"I ain't fucking with y'all man," he chuckled just as Chasney walked back over.

"Here. I got you a plate," she said, holding a plate out for Enzo to grab with a smile on her face.

Frowning, Harlem looked over the plate she had prepared and chuckled. "He doesn't like barbeque sauce on his ribs."

Yaz choked on her drink and Dreka animatedly beat on her back as she were dying. Enzo shook his head. The smile on Chasney's face immediately dropped. She didn't know if Harlem was trying to be funny or what, but her tone rubbed her the wrong way.

"That's weird. He's eaten it on a lot of things I've cooked for him."

The smirk on Harlem's face dropped this time. "And, that was in the past, sweetheart. Today's a new day."

Grabbing the plate from Chasney, Enzo shook his head. "It's cool. Thank you, Chas."

"Sure," she mumbled, walking away, back down to where his car was parked. Leaning against it, she released a deep breath to regulate her nerves. She too was regretting showing up with Enzo knowing her feelings for him weren't going anywhere overnight. But, she wasn't about to stand and argue about him liking barbeque sauce on his ribs or not. No, that would be absolutely absurd in her book.

"That's weird," Yaz mocked laughing. "I'm weak. This nigga Enzo, man."

"I ain't do shit. That's your girl always starting something with her moody ass," he said, casting his eyes down at her.

"I just thought the girl should know. I didn't do anything wrong."

"Yeah aight. Make that your last cup too."

Harlem looked up at him and cocked her head back. "Make this my what?"

"You heard what I said. Your ass is sitting down drinking and not gon' be able to walk when you stand up."

"Who said I planned on walking anywhere?"

Enzo's nose flared. It was no winning with her ass. "Good. Sit yo' ass still until I come back over here. I can tell by the way your thighs showing that you got on some little shit underneath that table. Don't get fucked up out here."

Harlem tossed her hand up at him, basically dismissing him. "Only person you need to be worried about is the chick you brought with you. I'm good, baby," she said easily.

"Yeah aight. You heard what I said," he hissed, walking away.

"And you heard what I said, nigga!" Harlem belted out, having to have the last word.

Her girls laughed while Enzo shook his head. He wasn't as hungry as Chasney had been, but he appreciated her for looking out on his plate.

"My bad about that," he somewhat apologized.

"It's fine. I just wasn't expecting her to say anything to me," Chasney replied. "Does she know about us?"

"Yeah and you know about her, so what you trying to get at? I'm single."

She rolled her eyes. "Clearly. I was just asking. I don't want any issues with her or her friends. We're friends and I just came out here to have a good time. That's it."

"Aight then, so get out your feelings. We good, aight?"

Chasney looked up at him and grinned. Enzo could do absolutely no wrong in her eyes. Nodding, she said, "Aight and I'm not in my feelings."

"Tell me anything, Chas," he chuckled.

Clearing her cup, Harlem yawned and stood from the table. She blinked her eyes a few times, realizing Enzo was right. Sitting down and drinking had been a bad decision. Laughing, her chin dropped to the center of her chest.

"I'm fucked up," she giggled.

"Oh, bitch, I know. You practically drank this fifth by yourself. Deep throat ass," Yaz jested.

Harlem stuck her tongue out and flicked it upward. "My nigga loves this deep throat too."

"That's your nigga now?" Dreka chuckled.

"Always was. Always will be."

Just as she staggered from behind the table, whoever was playing music turned on *Believe Dat*, by LightSkinKeisha. Dark liquor brought the ratchet side out of Harlem every time she drank it. Adding ratchet tunes to the equation was the recipe for her to shake her ass and show out.

"Here she go," Dreka laughed, watching Harlem swing her braids from side to side.

"Ayye. This my shit," Harlem said before holding onto the table and twerking her ass.

The shorts she had on were short as hell, and the material

was thinner. Her cheeks hung out as she put her hands on her knees and moved one ass cheek then the other.

"Face down, ass up, mask up. Either way make a nigga give that cash up!" she sang, standing up straight.

The crop top she was wearing stopped right above her belly button, showing off her stomach. She was in her own little world dancing when someone walked up behind her and whispered in her ear.

"You throwing that mufucka, ain't you?" Kartel asked, pressing his warm lips against her ear and grabbing her around the waist.

Knowing exactly who the voice belonged to, Harlem grinned and rolled her hips. "You know how I do."

When the DJ transitioned into *Back That Azz Up*, Harlem started showing the fuck out. Placing her hands on the table, she twerked on Kartel like she had done plenty of times while they were dating. Like the real hood rat she was when the song came on, Harlem swung her braids over her shoulder and smirked when Kartel's grip tightened around her waist.

"Nah. She wildin'," Lucci choked out in a chuckle, blowing smoke from his mouth.

Enzo's jaw clenched as he pushed himself up from the hood of his car. He could handle Harlem talking slick at the mouth, but seeing her shake her ass all over another nigga that wasn't him wasn't about to fly with Enzo. Striding with anger up the hill, Yaz, Dreka, and Mina were too busy twerking themselves to peep when Enzo approached the table. Shoving Kartel from behind her, he snatched Harlem up from the twerking position she was in.

"You want this nigga blood on your hands," he growled in her ear.

It wasn't a question. More like a statement that made goosebumps cover Harlem's arms. Swallowing hard, she jerked away from.

"You tripping," she hissed.

"We got a problem, my nigga?" Kartel spat, tugging on his jeans.

Enzo looked him over and smirked. "Nah. We ain't got shit, but if you got one, I won't hesitate to solve that muthafucka for you."

Harlem stepped to Enzo's side, sobering up just a tad. His tone of voice was nothing nice. The men stared one another down, not backing down until Kartel sucked his teeth.

"You can have that bitch. She ain't even worth it."

"Oh hell nah, pussy!" Yaz shouted, damn near jumping over the table.

Harlem moved to slap the shit out of Kartel, but Enzo grabbed her hand, yanking her to his side. If he put hands on Harlem, he was ending that nigga's life. He still might for disrespecting, but not right now. There were too many eyes watching them.

Smirking, Enzo grabbed Harlem around the waist and

palmed her booty with one hand. Shrugging, he said, "She was always mine."

Glaring at Harlem and realizing Enzo was the nigga she couldn't let go of for him, Kartel felt like a bitch. Harlem's teeth gritted as she mugged him.

"You're sad," she said, shaking her head.

She couldn't believe he had just come out the side of his neck like that, but could she blame him? Yes, he was dead wrong for calling her out of her name, but Harlem had strung him along like a ragdoll for years. At one point she did love him, but it was more so out of him being a support system than the man he was. Kartel was past fed up with Harlem's shit, but he didn't know how to let her go. If he wanted to keep his life, he'd use today as an example and erase everything about her from his memory.

When Kartel walked away, Harlem pushed Enzo off her. "You do too much," she hissed.

"Nah. I ain't did shit yet. Shoulda stayed sitting your ass down like I said, and we'd be good."

"You're not my man! Damn!" Harlem yelled.

"Harlem, chill. You doing too much," Dreka told her.

Huffing, she flopped down at the table. "I was minding my business and y'all wanna say *I'm* doing too much, like he didn't just walk his watermelon head ass up here fucking with me."

"Aye. You better watch your mouth," Enzo said calmly.

"I ain't gotta watch shit. Go pacify the chick you brought

and let me be," she said, twisting the cap on a cold bottle of water.

Enzo looked on as she thirstily downed the bottle and nodded his head. He wanted to do and say so much more, but he was going to let Harlem make it. The liquor clearly had her tripping, and before he said something reckless, he'd rather walk away.

"Aight. You got that, Harlem."

"I know I do. Bye," she said, shooing him away.

Yaz shook her head with a chuckle and Lucci grabbed her by the back of her neck. "The fuck you giggling for? You think that shit is cute?"

"Boy," she laughed. "Gone. You been acting like you got sense all day. Don't start because Enzo here."

"Whatever. You better not ever try to son me like that."

Blinking her long lashes, Yaz hit him with her killer smile. "Never, bae," she said, lying through her teeth.

If the opportunity presented itself, Yaz would be checking Lucci's ass too. These niggas wanted to get all upset when the roles were reversed, but were the ones starting shit. Enzo had a whole female posted up on his car with a dumb ass look on her face but was trying to check Harlem. The only thing he needed to be checking was the time on his watch, and realizing Harlem wasn't for his bullshit at the time.

"I can't believe Kartel just did all that," Dreka said, shaking her head.

"I can. It's Enzo who done ran me hot."

She stared straight ahead as Enzo typed away on his phone. When her phone vibrated on the table, she looked down, and of course, he had texted her.

That mouth of yours just got you in trouble.

Picking her phone up, Harlem sent him a bunch of middle finger emoji's and tapped the blue arrow to send them. Nodding, Enzo bit down on his bottom and looked up to where Harlem was sitting. She was staring back at him and rolled her eyes before turning to face Dreka. She wasn't about to go there again with him. It was bad enough they had put on a show for the people out there; going back and forth through messages was not about to happen.

All Harlem wanted to do was enjoy the rest of her day with her girls without all the unnecessary bullshit. Not knowing what Enzo was about to be on, Harlem snatched her phone up and blocked his number. Since he wanted to show out after going missing for days on her, Harlem was about to give him a taste of his own medicine.

Startled out of her sleep by the obnoxiously loud banging on her door, Harlem hopped out of her bed, cocking her gun back and rushed down the steps. Damn near falling on her face from missing the last step, she cursed and caught her balance. Unlocking the door, she snatched it open with a scowl on her face. Lowering her gun, she sucked her teeth.

"What, Enzo?"

He ran his tongue over the top row of his teeth, and pushed past Harlem, stepping inside the house. "Close the door, man. You ain't got no fucking pants on," he fussed.

"Obviously. I was fucking sleep," she mumbled lowly, closing the door with a lock following. Turning around, she frowned as Enzo stood there looking angry and sexy as hell. The mug on his face was making her pussy wet.

After the festivities at the park, Harlem was too drunk to do anything else but sleep her liquor off. Her friends made sure she was home safely before they headed to Lucci's crib where the party continued. Enzo had been amongst the crowd and waited until he was sure Harlem had slept her liquor off before popping up on her.

Enzo just stood there looking at Harlem. He couldn't believe how she showed her ass today. That was a side of her he hadn't witnessed either. Drunk Harlem was a loose cannon and he could only imagine how she used to behave back in the day. It couldn't have been anything nice.

"What you just standing there staring for?" she asked with attitude.

"You really like pissing me off, huh?"

Harlem rolled her eyes. "You piss yourself off thinking I'm about to move a certain way because that's what you want me to do. Sorry. I'm not."

"'Cause you fucking stubborn."

"What are you even here for? Don't you have company in town."

Enzo licked his lips and flopped down on the couch. "I dropped her ass off at the hotel."

"How fucking considerate," she scoffed, finally moving away from the door.

"Man," Enzo huffed, grabbing her arm as she tried walking by. "Bring your ass here."

"Mooove," she whined, trying to break free but it was no use.

Smacking her hard on the ass, Enzo stood up and tossed her onto the couch. "Nah. You had a lot of mouth on you earlier. Let me hear you talk that shit while this dick up in you."

Tugging his pants and boxers down, Enzo stroked his long dick before slapping it against Harlem's bare ass cheek after damn near snatching her panties to shreds.

"Enzo, wa-wait," she huffed, trying to lift up.

"Nah. Ain't no muthafuckin' wait," he spat, slapping her ass again.

Rubbing the tip of his dick against her lips, he bit his bottom lip easing inside her. It had been far too long since he was in between her thighs and it felt like home sweet fucking home once he was all the way inside.

Gripping the back of her neck, Enzo spread her legs apart with his knees, making Harlem arch her back more. Even if she didn't want to, she had no choice. Enzo had that type of dick that made Harlem want to cry it was so good.

"Ooooh, shit. Hold on!" Harlem cried as he stretched her tight walls out. He was getting reacquainted with his pussy again and loving it.

"Goddamn," he grumbled, delivering long, hard strokes.

"Enzo! My neck!"

Seeing how bent up he had her body, Enzo maneuvered them just a little, so she was facing the arm of the couch which was perfect for him. With one foot on the couch and the other planted on the ground, he grabbed ahold of Harlem's braids and beat her pussy out the frame.

"Oh my gooosh!" she moaned loudly. "You're toooo deep!"

"No, the fuck I ain't. Quit crying and take this dick with your stubborn ass."

Pounding into her, Harlem threw her ass back. Her ass cheeks jiggled every time their skin clapped together. Enzo tossed his head back and gripped her hips as she squeezed her pussy muscles. Enzo was trying to break her back in for the stunt she pulled earlier. Lifting her up by the waist, he stood her on her feet, spread her legs, forcing her to touch her toes all while still inside of her.

"You gon' learn to stop showing the fuck out," he growled, gripping her hips and slamming into her.

"Oooh. I am. I am. I promise."

"You are what?" he hissed, poking at her g-spot.

Harlem's mouth dropped open and her breath got caught in her chest. She couldn't even speak he was so deep. Bringing his hand around to her clit, Enzo massaged and stroked her simultaneously. The view of her from behind as she wet his dick up had him ready to nut. When her muscles clenched, his knees buckled.

"Ah, fuck."

Hearing his low groan of appreciation, Harlem wobbled her ass and placed her knees on the couch. Arching her back, her lower half laid across the couch as her backside moved fluidly up and down Enzo's dick.

"Mmm. I love this dick, baby," she moaned, feeling his dick twitch.

"Fuck. I'ma nut," he stressed, stroking deeper, longer, and quicker.

Meeting his thrusts, Enzo's toes popped in the Gucci slides he now had on and his back stiffened as he blasted off inside her. Breathing hard, he gripped Harlem's shoulder and shook his head before chuckling.

"Shit, I missed you," he admitted.

Harlem was sprawled out half awake. Hell, she felt her soul float away a while ago, so she was sure the shell of her body was the one he was talking to. Rolling over to her side, Harlem sat up on the couch and released a deep breath. Staring up at Enzo with his lip tucked between his teeth, Harlem grinned and grabbed his face between her hands.

"I missed you too," she said against his lips before kissing him.

Crossing her arms around his neck, Enzo scooped her up, and she wrapped her legs around his waist. They tongue wrestled as Enzo walked them up the steps to her bedroom. Gently, he laid her on the bed and entered her with one stroke. Kissing on her neck, Harlem gasped in awe at how he was able to get back hard that quickly. She just had that effect on him.

As he delivered slow strokes that had her tearing up, Harlem looked him in the eyes. Those honey-colored eyes that she fell in love with. He captivated Harlem from day one.

"I love you."

Enzo dropped his head into the crook of her neck. "I love you more."

His warm, minty breath tickled Harlem's skin, causing a chill to shoot up her spine. Regardless of what they went through, the love they had for one another would never waver. After making love, the two fell asleep almost immediately. Though Harlem had just woken up, she was in a dick induced sleep that had her lightly snoring when she didn't even snore.

It wasn't until early morning when the sun was rising that Harlem woke up again. The only reason she had peeled her eyelids open was because her phone was ringing off the hook. Enzo snatched it up from the dresser and was telling her to wake up as he answered her phone. It wasn't anyone but Dreka, but the way she was blowing her line down was about to piss him off. He was getting some good sleep.

"She sleep," he answered, annoyed as hell.

"Wake her up."

Nudging her, Harlem frowned and grabbed the phone out of his hand with her eyes back closed. "Huh?" she grumbled.

"Where you at?"

Harlem sucked her teeth. "At home, why?"

"Zeema and Ranisha were killed last night."

That had her eyes opening right on up. Glancing over at Enzo who had his back to her, she sat up some in the bed.

"Damn. For real? You know what happened?"

"Yeah. I guess she wasn't pregnant by ole boy after all," she revealed, causing a weird feeling to come over Harlem.

"One of his homeboys was her real baby daddy, and he busted in her house while they were there on some jealous type of shit. Killed them both and tried to flee the scene but the cops had already been called."

Harlem shook her head. "Damn. That's crazy. She hadn't even been home long."

"Right. You know everybody thinking she set ole boy up now," Dreka said, not wanting to say Trill's name.

A sigh of relief left Harlem's body. Though the heat behind his murder was never on her, it surely wasn't going to be now that the only witness was dead. Knowing the KCPD, they'd chalk it up as another unsolved murder, and claim it was a lover's quarrel gone deadly. It seemed they had better things to do than solve murder cases, like policing people for temporary tags when no one gave a fuck about those.

Yawning, Harlem eased back under the covers. "Well, Karma is a bitch. Did her baby survive?" she found herself asking.

"Nah. I don't think so. That nigga did the fool on her."

Her heart sank a little hearing that the baby hadn't made it. She knew all too well what it felt like to lose a child. She wasn't as far along as Zeema was, but the pain was still the same. A loss was still a loss.

"I'm sure it's all over social media. I'll have to look at it when I get up," she said, releasing another yawn.

"Mhm. Enzo must have worn your ass out," she snickered.

"Bye Dreka," Harlem chuckled before she hung up.

Putting her phone on the nightstand beside her, Harlem curled up behind Enzo and pressed her breasts against his warm back. Wrapping her arm around his waist, and leg over his thigh, she snuggled against him and kissed his back.

"Mmm. You're so warm," she cooed.

"And yo' hands cold as fuck," he grimaced as she rubbed her hand up and down his abs. "What time is it?"

"Almost nine. Dreka just told me Zeema and Ranisha were killed last night."

Enzo was silent for a second. He hadn't been made aware

that Vonzell was no longer babysitting her. Once Harlem did let Zeema go, she went straight to Ranisha's house and had been hiding out until last night. Her parents knew she was back home and no longer missing, but that was it. They made a public Facebook status updating everyone, and a few days later, she was killed in cold blood.

It was a cruel world out here, and she had lived it. Had it been up to Enzo, she would have been dead, but he let Harlem handle the decision making. Thankfully, the outcome was in their favor.

"She had it coming," he said, rolling over and laying on his back. "How you feeling?"

"Is it wrong to say relieved?"

Enzo shook his head no. "Nah. Had she crossed you again, who knows what would have happened."

He was right. Zeema had practically sealed her on death. Ranisha told her the day they ran into Harlem at the nail shop that she was going to get her ass killed one day for messing with all these different dudes, and she was right. The only thing was, Ranisha never thought she'd lose her life as well.

Having been friends with her, or what she assumed was a friendship, Harlem did feel a way. She couldn't understand how disloyal some females were built. Never in her life had she felt the need to be grimy to another woman, let alone people she considered a friend. Had Zeema been raised with some morals and known what it meant to be loyal, she'd possibly still be living.

"I'm fine. I just wasn't expecting that phone call."

Enzo kissed the tip of her nose. It was such an endearing act; one Harlem has loved since the first time he did it.

"Life comes at you fast, baby. You gon' make us some breakfast?"

"Absolutely not. After the way you showed out yesterday? Ha!" she laughed, rolling over. Enzo was right behind her, tickling her belly.

"You ain't gone do, what?"

"Stop! O-Oh my gooosh!" Harlem laughed, trying to break free.

Easing up on the tickles, Enzo gripped her around the waist. "Nah. You showed *your* ass yesterday. Almost made me catch a case, on my mama."

"You always putting something on your mama. I was only giving you the same energy you were giving me."

"Yeah? That's what that was?"

Harlem smirked, knowing he was about to get serious as hell. It was too early for all that. "Yes. So, don't lay here acting like you were all innocent either. How you just gone leave your company like that?"

She didn't really care about Chasney, but if she was in her shoes, Harlem knew she'd be pissed smooth off. A nigga had better never in his life fly her out and dip off with another bitch.

"She good. She texted me late last night about catching an early flight back this morning," he said, yawning all in Harlem's face before kissing on her neck.

"Un, un. Don't start this morning. I'm sore still. What were you drinking yesterday?"

Enzo grinned. "Hennessy."

"Should have known. You were fucking me for hours."

He kissed her neck again. "Nah. I was making love to this," he said cupping her pussy in the palm of his hand. "No shit; you probably got pregnant last night."

Harlem tensed up for a second and relaxed right after. "You think so?" she asked softly.

He eased his hand up her bare stomach and massaged her boobs. Enzo just had to touch on Harlem. It didn't matter where they were or what they were doing; he was showing his affection for her wherever. He was a man of words and actions that spoke a great magnitude of his love for Harlem.

"Yeah. If not, we can always keep trying."

Blinking back tears, Harlem cleared her throat and twisted her head, so their lips were practically touching. "You want a baby?"

Enzo nodded. "Mhm. From my baby," he said, kissing her lips and pulling her closer to him than she already was. "Only when you're ready, though. So, I'll just pull out next time."

She wanted to tell him he didn't have to, but instead just mumbled an okay. They lay there in silence for the next twenty minutes. Harlem's mind was on him wanting a baby, and Enzo's was on the next business move for himself. He had a meeting later on in the week with Meechi, a well-known cat throughout Kansas City. If anyone was living proof of making it out the game, he most certainly was. He had his own blueprint, and Enzo was just going to tweak it to meet his and Harlem needs.

Every move he made from here on out was for the both of them. Though he had bailed on her when she needed him the most, Harlem had never switched up on him. For that, Enzo was going to do his best to show her that there was more to life than taking from others. He had been scamming for so long; he knew preaching to her about the life she lived wasn't going to work, so he knew he had to come at her in a different angle. One that could set them straight for years to come. He just hoped Harlem wasn't too stuck in her 'get it how she lived' ways to be open for a change.

CHAPTER SEVEN

Strolling down the aisle in Walmart, Harlem had a smile on her face. She was happy for many reasons, but seeing her siblings always put her in a better mood. Bree and Davion were fighting over which bag of assorted chips they were going to get, and Harlem couldn't help but snicker.

"Nobody is even going to eat those nasty chips, Bree," Davion fussed.

"And no one wants hot chips. Just get a bag to yourself. Me and mama eat these all the time," Bree debated back.

"Since you can't decide, ask mama," Harlem said.

"Ma!" They screeched at the same time.

Andrea just shook her head as she rounded the corner. "Get one bag a piece. Y'all be going through bags of chips like crazy. Unless y'all know somebody with some food stamps, we're cutting back on the junk food."

"What's food stamps?" Bree asked, making Harlem chuckle.

"Something I wish I had. It's basically free money you get from the government to spend on food every month," she explained.

"Ooh. I want some of those too, then. How do we get them?"

The seriousness and innocence of her question had Andrea and Harlem chuckling. Bree wasn't well aware of the struggle, but had been exposed to it at a young age. Once Harlem got them into a nice neighborhood and school district after one too many shelters, Bree was green to a lot of the hardships Harlem faced. Davion, on the other hand, was well versed on what it was like to struggle. Some of his friends at school still did and he'd look out for them the way he knew his big sister would look out for him.

"When you get older, Bree Bree," Andrea chuckled, as her kids tossed two totally opposite bags of chips in the cart.

Heading to the aisle where the laundry detergent was, Andrea almost collided with another cart coming out of the aisle. Looking up ready to apologize, her eyes sparkled in recognition at the woman standing in front of her.

"Jasmyn?" Andrea called out.

"Andrea? Girl, oh my gosh," she squealed, stepping around her basket to hug Andrea. "How have you been?"

"I've been good. How are you?"

"Blessed, girl. I'll tell you that. Look at your babies," she gushed, eyes beaming with nothing but happiness. "Harlem. Girl, you done grew all the way up ain't you? How old are you now?"

"Twenty-four," Harlem answered, as they broke away from a hug.

Jasmyn still looked the same as she did years back. Harlem couldn't help but ogle over her fair skin tone that had no blemishes. She looked young enough to be Harlem's sister, rather than someone's mama.

"That's right. You're a year younger than Enzo," she said, giving her a smile that made Harlem's stomach churn. It was one of those 'I know you been fucking my son' smiles. Jasmyn was cool though and wouldn't dare call her out about it. Hell, she and Enzo were grown.

"How is he and your youngest son?" Andrea asked.

"Too much if you ask me, girl. I forgot how stressful raising a male teenager was."

"Tell me about it," Andrea said, reaching out to grab Davion, but he scooted away. "See what I mean?"

The mothers laughed, and Harlem looked on with a smile on her face. It had been so long since she saw her mother even hold a conversation with another woman, besides her aunt Chalise. Andrea and Jasmyn had kept in touch months after they were out of the shelter, but Andrea's depressive state caused her to shut the world out. Seeing how good and well put together Jasmyn was, her mind went to a sad place. *Had I not been so hung up over Dre, I'd look this good.*

"I love your hair," Jasmyn exclaimed, putting Andrea's insecurities on the back burner that quickly. There was nothing like one black woman complimenting another. It could simply make one's entire day.

"Thank you. Harlem had one of her friends braid it."

"They look good. We'll have to go out and catch up sometime. I'm glad to see you're doing good," Jasmyn said, giving her a genuine smile.

"You too. Let's exchange numbers. I need to get out of the house more."

Harlem's eyes widened at her response. She didn't know what had gotten into her mother, but she was glad to see her back to her normal self. Even if it was only for a few hours; progression of any kind was still good.

"It was good seeing y'all," Jasmyn said, scooting her basket along after they swapped numbers.

"You too," Andrea and Harlem replied as Bree waved bye.

After going through the long checkout line and packing their groceries and a few household items in the truck, they climbed inside. Harlem was the first to speak on the exchange between Andrea and Jasmyn.

"I think it'll be good for y'all to hang out."

Andrea glanced her way. "Really? Is that because you're dating her son?"

Harlem's head snapped her mama's way. "Who told you that?" she asked with a hint of laughter in her voice.

"Now you already know the snitch in this car," she laughed. "It wasn't Bree."

Harlem shook her head with a grin. One morning when she was taking Davion to school, Enzo had called her. They discussed plans for lunch and Harlem was just grinning. Them meeting up was simple, but any moment spent with Enzo put a smile on her face. Davion peeped the longing, loving look in his sister's eyes and chuckled.

"Was that Enzo from the shelter?" Davion asked once she pulled in front of his school.

She forgot all about the caller i.d. showing on the dashboard monitor. "Why, nosy?"

"Just asking. You must really like him. You been smiling the entire ride here," he told her.

"I do. Now bye. Have a good day at school and you better not be chasing behind none of these fast, little girls."

Davion waved her off. "They do the chasing. Not me."

Harlem grinned and released a deep sigh at her maturing little brother. Remembering that morning Enzo had called, she glanced in the backseat at Davion, who was nodding his head with Dre Beats covering his ears. He was in his own little world not knowing his mama had just snitched on him.

"We're not dating," Harlem replied.

"If you say so. It's okay if you are. I mean, I'm not getting any younger."

Harlem's face frowned up. "Are you asking for grandkids?"

"Bree is nine, about to be ten. I'm not asking; just throwing hints out there," she said, looking Harlem's way with a smirk plastered on her face.

Harlem didn't know how to feel about her not so subtle hint. The pregnancy topic hadn't been brought up in years and especially not since the miscarriage. Surprisingly, in the last couple of weeks, Andrea and Enzo had brought up her having kids. She didn't know if it was their emotions speaking for them or what, but they needed to chill.

"I'll let you know when I'm ready. Jasmyn still looks the same."

Andrea nodded. "She does. Had I not been so depressed, I'd probably look just as good as she does."

"Ma, stop. You are beautiful," Harlem said, grabbing her hand. "We're moving past all the sad stuff, remember?"

Nodding her head, Andrea squeezed Harlem's hand. "You're right. I just get caught up in my own thoughts sometimes."

"You don't have to apologize. Just promise me when Jasmyn calls, you'll go out."

Andrea smiled. "I can make that. Now, are you cooking tonight or me?"

Harlem laughed and snatched her hand away playfully. "Whew. All of a sudden I just got so sleepy."

Laughing, Andrea shook her head. She thanked God

every day for pulling her through some of the toughest days of her life. Harlem was hard on her, but it was for a reason. She knew her mama was stronger than what the devil was trying to convince her she wasn't. With a little encouragement and reminders of why her presence was needed, Andrea was slowly getting back to her old self.

The incident at the restaurant had almost made her double back and swallow down so many pills, but she remembered the look on Harlem's face when Kishana flashed her pills in the air. It was one of disappointment and disgust. A look she no longer wanted to receive. Andrea wanted to be the mother her kids deserved, and if that meant stepping out of the house with an old friend, then she was down for it.

"I'm proud of you," Harlem said as they pulled out of the parking lot.

Andrea's heart swelled. "Thank you, baby. I appreciate you more than you can imagine."

"I shouldn't be doing this shit, but oh well," Yaz said under her breath.

Her eyes darted to the entrance of the kitchen, before glancing back down at the phone in her hand. Nova's phone. He had left it on the kitchen counter over five minutes ago, and Yaz' curious senses started to tingle. She was never the type to go through a nigga's phone. In fact, she hardly got close to a guy long enough to care that much, but Nova was different.

She had been doing her dirt and fucking Lucci, but something deep down was telling her Nova had been doing his thing too. Checking his text messages wasn't her concern. Nova stayed swiping his long ass fingers against his screen, scrolling his Instagram newsfeed. She knew for a fact if he was up to anything, it'd be in his direct messages. Seeing the blue notification in the corner of his IG app with the number three encircled, Yaz took a deep breath and tapped on it.

The first message had her face screwed up. "The fuck do she mean, did he get the money she sent him?" she hissed, opening the unread message.

Quickly, with the expertise of an investigator, Yaz read over their most recent messages. Figuring the two had been in contact for a while, she scrolled to the top of the messages, and her eyes bulged out of their sockets at the date. It was from over a year ago. Well before Lucci had gotten out of jail, and way before Yaz even thought about cheating on Nova.

"This muthafucka," she spat, tossing the phone onto the counter, ready to confront him.

Turning around, she jumped a little seeing him standing in the doorway. Nova was fine. The type of fine Yaz normally stayed away from, but he had somehow charmed her into being his girl. Standing at six foot even, bright skin tone with a red hue to it, a clean-cut, thick beard adorning his face and even bigger dick in his pants; Nova was a lot of women's dream man. And, by the looks of it, he had been making their dreams come true.

"You find what you were looking for?" he asked smoothly.

Yaz tossed a hand on her hip. "You a dirty muthafucka, you know that? Nah, I know you know that. Your ass been cheating on me this entire relationship. I can't believe you."

"I don't know why this is a shock to you."

Yaz' eyelids stretched wide. "What?! The fuck do you mean, you don't know why? Maybe because we're in a relationship and cheating is nowhere in the terms of this arrangement."

"You barely pay any attention to me, Yaz," he chuckled and stepped inside the kitchen. "Now you wanna act surprised when a nigga steps out on you. If it makes you feel any better, it was only one person."

Yaz' head snapped back so far; she damn near broke her neck. She couldn't grasp what Nova was saying right now. He was speaking nonchalantly as if what he was saying was cool. As if they had been having issues in their relationship and that made it okay for him to step out on her. Yes, she was being a hypocrite, but Nova didn't know that.

"Are you serious right now?" she asked, feeling silly for even asking because she knew without a doubt he was.

"Dead serious. Look Yaz. You know a nigga fucks with you, but you are spoiled, ma. Too damn spoiled. Everything doesn't revolve around you, and sometimes a nigga just wants to feel wanted for more than the money he throws your way."

"Nigga, I don't need your fucking money! I'm your girlfriend; you're supposed to spoil me!" she shouted.

"Nah. Not when my efforts aren't appreciated. I don't know if it's due to you having daddy issues or what, but I'm good on us."

She struggled to swallow the lump in her throat. Yaz' didn't have daddy issues. There was no daddy to even complain about. Not one she had saw in years anyway. For Nova to try and throw that in her face, was practically him slapping her.

"So, you get caught red-handed and now wanna claim you're good on us? Pussy, I put you on. I upgraded your pockets and you wanna try to stunt on me?" she asked, cocking her head to the side.

When they first met, Nova was doing a little hustling in the streets, but he hadn't really made a name for himself. Being the supportive girlfriend that she was, Yaz hooked Nova up with her cousin Petey, who lived in The Dubs. He was getting money hand over fist and could've been moved out the hood, but it was just that. His hood. Since his cousin had put in a good word for Nova, Petey put him on in more ways than one and had his pockets sitting lovely. Yaz had never in her life been an Indian giver, but right now, she was wishing she had never put Nova on.

"I could've let your ass starve and not make any moves on any blocks, and you wanna come at me like that?" She asked and chuckled. It was a chuckle of disbelief and irony. She was so shocked by this nigga; it was actually humorous.

Nova sucked his teeth. "Man, your ass didn't put me on shit. I knew that nigga Petey well before I started fucking with you."

"But I brought you around him not knowing you were just a fucking opportunist. Is that why you stuck around? Trust me, if you been wanting to leave, you could have done so. I'm not pressed over no nigga. I don't need no nigga. I'm what a nigga needs."

"And that's your fucking issue!" Nova spat, getting pissed off. "You act like I'm not good enough for you. Like you don't need a nigga, so I got me a bitch who does."

"Well, go be with that bitch then, Nova! Bye!" Yaz yelled, with her nose flaring.

"You want me to leave so bad 'cause you probably been fucking around too," he said, clenching his jaw.

"And, nigga if I was? Clearly, I've been single this entire time, so it wouldn't matter now would it?"

The two stared one another down. Nova was daring her to admit that she had fucked around on him. He wanted to play like she had bruised his ego, but Yaz didn't give a fuck.

He knew from jump the type of female she was. From day one, she had never been or showed him anything but the real her. It was his fault for thinking he could change her. Truth be told, Yaz had changed some for him and that's why her feelings were a little hurt. He was talking bad to her like she hadn't been shit their entire relationship. She had only recently started cheating, though.

The sound of knocks at the door made them break their stare down. Seeing him not make a move to answer it, Yaz sucked her teeth and stomped out of the kitchen. Not bothering to look out the peephole, she pulled the door open and damn near fell out once her eyes landed on the visitor.

"The fuck you looking all surprised for?" Lucci fussed, with a small grin on his handsome face.

"What are you doing here?" she hissed trying to shut the door.

"I told you what was gon' happen the last time you ignored me," he said while brushing past her and stepped inside the house.

The day of the barbeque, Lucci had played nice all evening, and Yaz finally knew why when she saw him hugged up with another female. It was just some chick he used to fuck on, but it didn't matter to Yaz. Even after the barbeque when some people went back to his crib to kick it, the same girl had Lucci's attention. Normally, Yaz would have went off on him right then and there, but one of Nova's homeboys was in attendance. The last thing she wanted to do was be seen causing a scene over another nigga that wasn't hers.

Instead, Yaz left and blocked Lucci's number. With having been out of town for business purposes for the last week and a half, he hadn't had time to address the issue at hand. Now, was that time though. Or so he thought.

"Who the fuck is this nigga?" Nova bellowed in confusion.

"You might wanna pipe the fuck down, my G. This ain't got nothing to do with you," Lucci replied calmly. He was calm, but the grit in his tone made a chill shoot through Yaz' entire body.

"You fucking this nigga?" Nova spat in Yaz' direction. "Got this nigga popping up at your crib and shit. That's what you on?"

"You've been cheating on me our entire relationship, Nova. If anyone should be upset, it should be me."

"Nah. You ain't got no reason to be upset. That's what you hoes do, right? Wanna flip the script on a nigga 'cause you weren't doing your part in the relationship so now I'm the bad guy."

"Hoes?" Yaz said, still stuck on his choice of words. She was far from a hoe. Much too far for him to be throwing that word around so loosely.

"Yeah. That's exactly what I said."

"That's fine. I'll be a hoe, because you know what? Hoes like me could've been done with your ass, but nah, I stuck around. Since you want to claim I fucked him, I did," she said, tossing her hands in the air. "Yep. Sure did. Right outside in *my* mothafuckin' driveway while your punk ass was upstairs counting sheep, when your broke ass should've been dreaming about money," she laughed but stopped when a sting so sharp graced the side of her face.

Before he could take his next breath, Nova had a gun to his head and fear in his eyes. Lucci had snatched his gun from his waist so quick; he didn't even blink.

"I should blow your fucking brains out right now, bitch. Give me a reason not to," he gritted through clenched teeth.

Shocked was an understatement of what Yaz was feeling. Though her face stung like hell, her heart was beating out of her chest thinking she was about to witness a homicide. She was certain this wasn't on her bucket list.

"Lucci. Let him go. It's not worth it. He's not worth it," she pleaded, grabbing hold of his arm.

Yaz' frightened tone pulled him out of the dark place he had traveled to. He was still on papers, and though he could've more than likely gotten away with killing Nova, he wasn't taking any chances. It didn't mean he couldn't beat his ass, though. Backing away from him, Nova let out a sigh of relief just as the butt of Lucci's gun connected with his nose, cracking it on impact.

"Arrrgh! Fuck, man," he groaned, holding his now twisted and leaking nose.

Lucci bashed him over the head with the gun, wanting to knock him out. Blood dripped profusely onto Yaz' wood floors, and she almost caught an attitude about it but stopped. Lucci had smacked Nova across the face for disrespecting her. He didn't have to do that, so she checked herself real quick.

"Get the fuck out her crib. If I see you over here again,

you gone come up missing," Lucci hissed pushing him toward the door before kicking him in the ass.

Nova stumbled out of the house, tripped over his feet, and tumbled down a few steps, unable to break his fall. Yaz slapped a hand over her mouth in awe at the scene playing out in front of her.

"Oh my gosh," she whispered once the door was closed.

Licking his lips, Lucci turned to her and grinned. "You wanna ignore me again?"

Shaking her head, Yaz laughed and stepped over to him. Snatching him to her by the front of his shirt, Lucci smacked her round booty and held it while she looked up at him.

"You are crazy, you know that?"

"Yeah. I've been told a time or two," he smirked. "You like this crazy shit, huh?"

Embarrassed to admit it aloud, Yaz just nodded her head. "I don't know why."

"Nah. You and I both know why."

Smashing his lips into hers, Yaz gasped before letting out a satisfied moan. Right there in her living room with blood on her floor, a gun in his hand, and her with a red cheek; the two tongued each other down like they had not an issue in the world. In Lucci's eyes, they didn't have any issues. Not anymore at least.

Pulling away from the kiss first, Yaz tucked her bottom lip into her mouth. Her eyes sparkled with lust at how fine Lucci looked in this moment and before. His hair had grown back drastically and was braided into two braids to the back. The gold and diamond bottom grill shined brightly, and it better had with the money he dropped on the mouthpiece.

He had a crazed look in his eyes that made Yaz' pussy and heart beat in a synchronized manner. No guy she ever messed around with in the past made her feel the way Lucci did. Tired of fucking with the lames she had stumbled across, Yaz made up in her mind right then and there that Lucci's thuggin' ass was just what she needed. Jumping fresh out a situation into another was risky, but Yaz was all about taking risks. The way Lucci had her mind racing and stomach fluttering, she was ready to risk it all.

CHAPTER EIGHT

Squinting her eyes at the screen of her MacBook, Harlem released a frustrated sigh. She had been looking up college classes to take for over an hour now and she was over it. The only reason she was even interested in going back was because of Enzo, who was sitting next to her on the couch watching TV.

"What's wrong?" he asked.

Poking her lips out, Harlem placed the MacBook on the glass table in front of her. "This shit is for the birds. What is a degree *really* going to do for me?"

"Whatever you want it to do," he chuckled, and she punched him the arm.

"I'm serious. I don't see the point in me going back to school now. Do you know how many successful people I know who dropped out of college or never went?"

Enzo nodded. "Yeah, but do you know them personally? Just 'cause you see these social media mufuckas making money and starting businesses without any college education, doesn't mean that's everyone's path. What field do you even wanna go into?"

Harlem sighed heavily and licked her lips. Only Enzo could frustrate and motivate her all in the same breath.

"I thought about business, but then I started researching counseling professions. You know I had to go to counseling back in the day."

"Word?"

That was news to Enzo, but he wasn't surprised though. Harlem had been through a lot. Nodded her head, she continued.

"Yeah. It was only for a few months, but I liked it. I had someone who didn't know me at all just listen to understand what I was going through and not judge me. I know there's tons of young girls just like me who probably are going through some of the same things. I could just talk to them, you know?"

Enzo nodded, understanding completely. "Yeah. I think that's dope, baby. I think you need a degree to counsel, though."

"I knooow," she groaned. "It'll be worth it, though. What you think?"

Hitting her with his handsome grin, Enzo leaned over and kissed her cheek. "I think you can do whatever you put your mind to. Go for that shit. There's lots of girls who need role models; why not you? You're already a great example for Bree."

"Really?" She asked softly.

Pulling her onto his lap, Enzo nodded his head and rubbed her back. "Yeah, shorty. She doesn't see you as the tough girl you be trying to act like you are," he said, chuckling as she crossed her arms over her chest. "She just sees you for Harlem. Her big sister who's had her back forever and loved her like she was her own child. You're perfect, baby."

Smiling, Harlem leaned forward and pecked his lips. Once, twice, and a third time. Enzo knew the right words to reassure her, even when he didn't know where they came from half the time. He was speaking nothing but facts though. The fact that she was even considering letting go of the lifestyle she was living, had Enzo's dick hardening and love for her growing even more.

"Look at you being so supportive," she giggled, trying to climb off his lap.

"Hol' up. Where you going? Look what you did." Pulling his shorts down some, his dick damn near popped out, making Harlem laugh.

"I have to get dressed. I'm taking Bree out for a girl's day."

"Let me take y'all out. My treat," he offered.

"Or, you could just give me the money."

"Nah. Let me spoil y'all," he said with a lick of his lips.

Enzo felt solely responsible for why Bree didn't have a

father in her life. His feelings for Harlem grew much stronger after she revealed all she had been through. He hated that she and her family had gone through what they had gone through, but he wondered what would have happened had Dre still been alive. Or, had he not called Harlem that night. Thoughts of her getting murdered by her mama's abusive boyfriend was all he thought about after it all went down. Thankfully, he was in the right place at the right time.

"Okay. I guess I can do that," Harlem said with a smile.

"Bet. What time we leaving?"

"Around twelve. It's ten thirty now," she said, and a sneaky grin covered Enzo's face. Harlem went to protest knowing why he was giving her that look but Enzo quickly stood to his feet. Playfully, he bounced her up and down as if she was riding his dick and kissed on her neck.

"That's plenty time to get you right," he grumbled, walking up the steps.

Harlem moaned out her agreement. He spoiled her in more ways than one and would be for as long as he was walking this earth.

"Is my sister your girlfriend?" Bree questioned Enzo as they sat at the table.

Harlem was sure Bree would want to hit up Charming Charlies, Build A Bear, and other girly stores, but she was wrong. The new bumper and race car track the city had opened was how she chose to spend the last portion of their day. Enzo was taken back a bit by her question but answered it anyway.

"What'd she tell you she was?"

Bree smiled innocently and shrugged her shoulders. "She didn't say anything. I'm asking you."

Laughing, he shook his head. Bree was indeed mature for her age, but kids her age were very inquisitive.

"Yeah. I'm her boyfriend," he answered.

Bree's eyes widened in excitement. "Really?"

Enzo nodded. "Really."

"Really what?" Harlem asked, sitting back down at the table. She had gone to get their tickets for the bumper cars since they were in her name.

Bree glanced at Enzo with lifted brows and he gave her a wink. "Nothing. Was just telling Bree we can stop for ice cream on the way home." Bree's eyes really lit up then.

"Yeah. We can do that. You ready to play?" Harlem grinned and Bree hopped up from her seat.

"Yes! Let's go, Enzo."

"Enzo? I thought we were playing," Harlem said with a pout.

Standing to his feet, Enzo kissed Harlem on her cheek and shot her a smile. "You got next, bae. You ready, Bree?"

"Yes! Yes!" she squealed.

Shaking her head with a smile on her face and swooning

heart, Harlem followed behind the duo as Bree ran full speed to the line. Seeing the excitement on her sister's face was all Harlem wanted to see. The fact that Enzo was also the cause for her beautiful smile had Harlem's feelings in shambles. If it ever got revealed that he was the reason Bree didn't have a father, she didn't know what'd she do. She now understood how Enzo must have felt when she didn't want him to leave. Conflicted with the man she loved and family she wanted to protect, Harlem prayed their secret never came to light.

Two hours later, Enzo was pulling up to Harlem's crib with Bree knocked out in the backseat. Peeking behind her, Harlem smiled softly and looked Enzo's way.

"You wore my baby out. Look at her."

Turning around, Enzo chuckled at the slob sitting in the corner of Bree's mouth. She was lightly snoring, and it reminded him of Harlem when she'd be knocked out cold in his bed at the shelter.

"She had a good time, though."

"She did. Thank you for hanging with us today. I had fun too," she said, leaning over to kiss the corner of his mouth.

"Maybe we can have our own little date soon. You be having a nigga cooped up in the house like you afraid to be seen out with me."

Harlem waved him off with a chuckle. "Oh, whatever. You know you be on the go, but we can definitely do that. How 'bout you fly me out of town like you were boasting about a few months ago?"

"You got a passport?" he asked smoothly.

It wasn't shit for Enzo to fly her anywhere she wanted to go. Harlem was easy to please. Though she had been wined and down by some of the wealthiest men she had come across, she was still modest. Especially when it came to Enzo. They both had come from practically nothing. Enzo could have bought her a brochure with the most extravagant countries throughout it and she'd play along like they had traveled to them before. With him, life seemed to be much easier to deal with. An unknown weight had been lifted from her shoulders and Enzo helped push it far away from them.

"Yes. I have one."

"Aight. Look up some flights and shit to where you wanna go. Nah. Matter fact, I'll do that. You just pick out some skimpy little outfits to wear," he said as his mind began to swarm with images of Harlem running around a villa with nothing but a thong on. He grinned and looked her way.

"What?" Harlem asked shyly.

"You beautiful as fuck."

Swallowing hard, Harlem felt like the young seventeen-year-old girl Enzo first encountered. She was so feisty yet shy when they first met. Enzo had truly turned her the fuck out, but Harlem didn't mind it one bit.

"Thank you. You aren't too bad yourself," she giggled.

"Shit. You know I ain't bad at all. You ready to go inside?"

She wasn't really ready to go in, but she felt herself growing tired as well. Nodding, she unclicked her seatbelt.

Enzo scooped Bree up from the backseat while Harlem grabbed all the bags she had collected over the day. Walking in the house, Enzo headed to the room Harlem transformed into Bree's little palace whenever she stayed over. She had her own room, while Davion slept in the guest room when he did visit.

Standing in the doorway, Harlem looked on with admiration as Enzo carefully laid Bree down. He was so gentle with her, Harlem couldn't help but wonder what'd he be like when they had a child.

"You good?" he asked, breaking her from her thoughts.

"Yeah. Just thinking how you would look with a baby in your arms."

Smiling, Enzo wrapped his arm around her waist and walked them out of the room toward the living room. Placing a hand on her stomach, Harlem surprised herself when she didn't tense up. *What the hell?* She thought.

"You want a little Enzo Jr. running around here?" he asked with a smile.

"No girl?"

"The Lord knows I'd act a fucking fool with a girl," he stressed, shaking his head. Harlem giggled. "I'm good with whatever he blesses us with, though. I got one blessing; I just need another to carry on our legacy."

Harlem's heart swelled. When he said shit like that, she was reminded why she loved him so much. Running her hands over his thick head of waves, she wrapped her arms around his neck. "Let me plan this trip and I'll think about it."

"Straight up?"

"Straight up," she snickered.

"Can we try right now?" Palming her booty in the leggings she was wearing, he cocked his head back. "You getting thick than a muthafucka."

Harlem tried pushing his hand away, but he just cupped her ass with both hands and squeezed harder.

"I know. I need to go on a diet. Exercise or something," she huffed, and Enzo shook his head.

"Nah. Ain't nothing wrong with your body. I love it, baby," he said, kissing on her neck.

"Un, un. Don't start. We were almost late earlier thanks to you."

Before picking up Bree, Enzo was sexing Harlem as if he had never done so before. Up against the shower wall, he ate her pussy like a straight beast and fucked her with such expertise, Harlem had tears sliding down her face. Enzo was relentless when he slid in between her legs as if he were making up for lost time.

"I can't help that I'm addicted to you," he said, smoothly licking his lips. "Give me a kiss so I can shake."

Obliging to his command, Harlem stood on her tippy toes and tongued her man down. Moaning in his mouth, she savored the taste of him to her memory. As good as Enzo's dick was, Harlem was dog tired and just wanted to shower before climbing in the bed.

"You telling me not to start and look at you," Enzo jested, rubbing his thumb across her bottom lip and pecking them again. "Come lock up."

"Okay," she mumbled.

Before he made it to the door, Enzo pulled out some money from his pocket and handed it to Harlem. She gave him a quizzical look, and he gave her one right back until she realized what it was for; their trip.

"Thank you," she said appreciatively. She was about to do the fool at the mall. As if she didn't have a closet full of threads with tags still on them.

"You're welcome. I'll hit you up later 'cause I know your ass about to take a nap," he chuckled and she nodded.

"You know me so well."

Harlem watched as Enzo jumped in his car and pulled out of the driveway. Letting out a yawn, she closed the door with a lock and set her new alarm Enzo bought her. He wasn't about to have her out here with the shit the people who lived here before her, considered to be security. Whenever someone was within a foot away from her front door, she received an alert on her phone.

Walking to her bedroom with a smile on her face, Harlem finally felt some kind of normalcy in her life. Going to her bathroom, she pulled her shirt over her head and turned to the side in her floor length mirror. Placing a hand on her stomach, she poked her belly out and giggled. She had eaten good at the racetrack and had a food baby. All that baby talk Andrea and Enzo had done over the last few weeks had her imaging herself carrying a child.

"If I look like this and I only ate, I can imagine what I'd look like with a real baby in here," she said, examining her frame once more before starting the shower.

A baby was a blessing, but Harlem knew she wasn't quite ready for that stage of life yet. She still needed to figure out what she was going to do about school. Sighing, she thanked God for even having options. Years ago, college was the last thing on her mind, let alone being a voice for young girls like her. It was amazing how He worked things out in her favor and she'd forever be grateful.

"Hi, my Sailer boo," Yaz cooed into her camera.

She and Sarena were on FaceTime catching up and Sailer had just woken up. Going on four months, she was still in the stages of waking up through the middle of the night, and with the move, Sarena was having a hard time adjusting to the time change. It was a little after noon in Kansas City, and seven in the evening over in Sweden.

Sailer let out a yawn and Sarena grinned like the proud mama she was. "She about to be up all night, now."

"You struggling to adjust?"

"Yes. It's the time difference that throws me off so bad. Other than that, I'm enjoying it. Marquis seems to love it here too."

"Well, I miss y'all. Harlem mentioned something about taking a trip so we'll see. Maybe for Christmas," Yaz suggested and Sarena nodded, enthused as ever.

"Yes! Christmas would be the perfect time. I'm going to start looking up stuff for us to do once we get off the phone."

"Who you in here talking to?" Lucci asked, jumping on top of Yaz while she lay on her stomach.

"Lucci! You are too heavy," Yaz groaned.

Rolling off her, he smacked her ass in the shorts she was wearing and smiled into the camera at Sarena. "What up? That baby girl with you?"

Sarena nodded and put the camera on Sailer. "Yep. Live and alert, trying to see what she can see."

Lucci grinned. "She's pretty as hell."

"Thank you. Yaz, I'ma call Harlem before Sailer gets too fussy. Love you. I'll send you details about the things we can do while y'all are here."

"Okay. Love you too. Send me some more pics of my boo too. You be acting stingy."

Giggling, Sarena told her she would, and they hung up. Connecting her phone back to the charger, Yaz rolled on her side and stared at Lucci with his fine ass. The two braids in his head were messy, showcasing his nice grade of hair, thanks to his mama's side. His eyes were red-rimmed, and the air now smelled of the exotic weed he had been puffing on minutes before. It was a mixture of his cologne as well, and it had Yaz taking a deep inhale. With a slow blink, he licked his juicy lips causing Yaz' pussy to jump.

"You staring like you ready to jump on a nigga," he chuckled.

"I'm just admiring you. Can I do that?" Yaz said, trying not to crack a smile.

"Maaan, watch out," he said, mushing her head. "You can admire something else while you laying here looking all good, shit."

Gripping his dick through his shorts, Yaz eyed his thick pole and licked her lips. As badly as she wanted to suck him off, they needed to get some things understood.

"Let's go get tested together."

"Aight when?"

Lucci so readily agreeing to her suggestion shocked her. Not because she expected him to say no, but because she expected him to argue with her about how he was clean and a whole bunch of other shit. Other men in her past gave her backtalk when she mentioned getting tested.

"Sometime this week. I'm not sucking anything until then," she said with a shrug.

"Okay?" he said, reminding her of the Waka Flocka meme. "I ain't eating that little pussy then either. So now what?"

"You are so childish," she said, laughing.

"What made you ask that? You trying to tell me something?"

Shoving his shoulder, Yaz rolled her eyes. "No, nigga. I just want to be sure we are both safe. I done let you hit raw like twice already and I know you be doing your thing or whatever, but if we're about to get serious, I want to make sure you're in good health."

"Who said anything about us getting serious?" he asked, brows furrowed together in utter confusion.

Yaz punched him in his arm. "What you think we're doing?"

"Aye. You better keep them hands to your muthafuckin' self. I ain't know that's what we was on," he said, scratching his head and sitting up on the bed.

"I don't know what you thought *I* was doing but, you think I'm just playing house with you for no reason? Nigga, you are mine."

Lucci shook his head and laughed. He was too high for this serious ass conversation. "Nah. I'm on parole. I belong to the state until further notice."

Yaz punched him in the arm again. "You really get on my fuckin' nerves. I'm 'bout to go home."

Seeing that she was serious, Lucci snatched her up around the waist, cradling her from the side. Any other chick he would have told to not let the door hit her on the way out, but Yaz was different. Their bond was different. It was rare for a female who wasn't dating a nigga to hold him down while in jail, let alone while in a relationship. Lucci had come across many disloyal mufuckas in his lifetime and out of all the females he had encountered before, and after jail, Yaz was the most solid one. He had a little chick on the under he was fooling around with, but she wasn't fucking with Yaz at all.

"You always trying to leave when you don't get your way," he hissed, biting her neck.

"It's my way or no way."

Lucci sucked his teeth. "You got me fucked up."

Lifting up, he towered over Yaz' thick frame and admired her chocolate thighs as they jiggled. Her nipples were rock hard in the tank top she was wearing, and Lucci's mouth watered from wanting to suck on them. He wanted to suck on something else too, though. Licking his lips, he gripped the top of her shorts and pulled them off before tossing them to the side.

"You fine as fuck," he spoke lowly, drinking her in.

"I know, nigga. Now give me some dick."

Reaching for his hardened member, Lucci smacked her hand away. "Lay your ass back and spread them legs for me."

Yaz' breath got caught in her chest, but she didn't miss the hunger in Lucci's eyes at all. Laying back, she spread her legs and sucked in a deep breath. Giving head wasn't Lucci's specialty.

He could give it, but most women he fucked with only got the dick and were satisfied. Had they known he was a pussy connoisseur, they'd wish he placed his tongue on them. It was something about Yaz, though. Hell, it was everything about her that had Lucci wanting to go the extra mile to please her. And, that he did. Using his hands, he spread her puffy lips and sucked on her clit.

"Oh ssss," Yaz hissed as her back inched off the bed some.

Rapidly flicking the tip of his tongue on her pearl, Yaz blinked to make sure she wasn't dreaming. Pushing her legs back more, Lucci covered her entire sex with his warm, juicy mouth and made loud slurping noises as he ate her up. Yaz' eyes rolled to the back of her head as she felt herself about to come that quickly.

"Luuuucci," she moaned out. "You're gonna make me cum. Fuck!"

Sliding two fingers inside her, he swirled them around in her wetness before locating the cushioned section he loved to probe at while deep inside her. Doing his fingers in a 'come here' motion, Yaz' legs' began to shake before clasping around his wrist.

"Nah. Open them fucking legs," he muffled, shoving her thigh down.

Diving his head back between her thighs, Lucci sucked hard on her clit while still stroking her g-spot. Yaz tried scooting away from him and she had never run from head in her life. *Oh nah. This nigga is crazy crazy,* she thought, hurriedly pushing him away.

Lucci looked up with a grin on his face. "Chu' running for?"

"No. You are not about to have me around here crazy. You eat every chick's pussy this good?"

Crazy thoughts swarmed Yaz' mind just thinking of him pleasuring another female like he had just done her. She could see herself busting out windows, doing pull ups, throwing clothes out and all. Shaking her head, she closed her eyes and sighed. That gave Lucci just enough time to have her back in the spot where he wanted her.

"Nah. Only you. Now quit playin' wit' me."

"You gon' make me crazy," she whispered out in a warning as he dropped his head back between her thighs and delivered a long, torturous stroke to her center.

"Good. I like my bitches coo coo," he chuckled, before sucking on her clit like it was his favorite piece of candy.

In a minute flat, he had Yaz yelling at the top of her lungs just like he knew she would be. All that talk about her going home was out the fucking window. If she wanted to leave, he'd let her now. But, he'd guarantee she'd have her ass right back over before he could miss her. Lifting up from her center as her legs shook uncontrollably, Lucci looked on with a smirk on his face as if he were watching her soul leave her body. When she finally peeled her eyes open and stared up at him, Yaz felt like she had just signed her life over to a maniac.

"Let's go get some food," Lucci said with ease, smacking her thigh.

She sat silent for a while, unable to speak. That tongue lashing left her speechless. Closing her eyes shut again, Yaz counted backwards from five before opening them again. She needed to gather her bearings before she embarrassed herself and told that nigga she loved him on some wild shit.

"Okay," she replied in a mumble.

"You good?"

Lucci tried to hit her with a serious expression, but the smirk he seemed to keep on his face in her presence wouldn't let up. Yaz had to muster up a lie. She couldn't let him know that he had snatched her soul from her body and damn near brought tears to her eyes. No. That'd boost Lucci's cocky ego even more.

"I'm fine."

"Yeah, you is fine than a muthafucka but get yo' ass up out my bed so we can go eat. I'm hungry as hell."

"You haven't had enough to eat?" Yaz replied seductively with a smirk as she licked her lips.

"Unless that pussy can fry some chicken, hell no," Lucci laughed and climbed from the bed. "Get yo' ass up!"

Sighing with a smile on her face, Yaz laid back on the bed and stared up at the ceiling. This thing between her and Lucci wasn't what she expected. After he went all savage on Nova, Yaz found herself removing him from her block list and developing feelings. Feelings she knew damn well she shouldn't have. Lucci wasn't the only one who appreciated their bond, that was mental way before physically; Yaz did too. She only hoped whatever they called themselves doing didn't make her look like a fool.

CHAPTER NINE

"I know I'm new to the legit business side of things, but I appreciate you for looking out," Enzo said, slapping hands with Meechi.

"Why learn some shit if you aren't going to be willing to share it later? Too many people have that crabs in a bucket mindset. If you aren't an enemy of mine, and you good people, I don't see why we can't help each other eat. Shit, I know I ain't gone ever starve so I might as well pass the plate," he chuckled but was dead serious.

Meechi had been in the drug game for years. He was born into it, thanks to his pops BM, and had passed it along to his cousin Sensay, who in turn shared the wealth with his prodigy Juvie. He still had a hand in shipments, but for the most part they had come in the game, stamped their name as some legends, and bowed out without a glitch. Well, there were a few over the years, but it had been so long since then.

"Yeah. I hear you on that. I'ma look into the business proposals you told me about and go from there. Me and my girl trying to really go legit," Enzo grinned just at the mention of Harlem.

"Make sure that homefront is solid. She a real one?"

Enzo nodded. "Realist female I've ever met. Shit, she practically the female version of myself," he chuckled and Meechi grinned.

"Well, you ain't got shit to worry about. Your mindset and hustle is going to take you far, Enzo. Just stay focused and remember what you are really doing this for. The money is something you can always get too. Your time? That can't be replaced, so move smart. You got my number if we need to link up again."

"Yeah. I got it. I wanna holla at Juvie when he gets some free time," Enzo said.

"I'll let him know. Matter of fact," he said, pulling his phone out. "Shoot that nigga a text so y'all can link up. I already told him who you were."

Enzo nodded. "Good lookin' out. Let me get out of here. My girl probably wondering where I'm at."

"Aight, man. Be safe."

"Always. You too."

Hopping in his ride, Enzo pulled out of the parking lot of *Juvie's*. The lounge had been up and running for a couple of years now and was still pulling in more than decent money. With them having a second lounge now open and Meechi being part owner, Enzo was glad Grady had connected him to some people who were clearly about their business.

On his way home, Enzo stopped by the grocery store and picked up Harlem some ginger ale. She had been complaining about a stomach ache all day and was knocked out when Enzo left for his meeting a few hours ago. For the past few weeks, Harlem had been staying the night at Enzo's place. He lived far out, but neither of them could go to sleep without one another in the bed with them. They would always fall asleep side by side or spooning, and somehow throughout the night, Harlem would maneuver her way on top of Enzo. She loved sleeping on top of him and had been for a while now. Enzo chuckled, finding it cute of her.

Pulling into the garage of his home that housed five bedrooms, four bathrooms, a theater, office space, and a larger than he needed it to be kitchen, Enzo released a content sigh as the door lowered. For as long as he could remember, he had dreamed of owning a nice home. Something he could invite his family over to and let them stay the night if they'd like.

His grandma, Candace stayed reminding him of patience. Enzo never had it growing up. If he wanted something done or needed something and no one could get it for him right then, he'd figure a way to get it. That was the hustler in him. The go-getter in him had paid off nicely.

Stepping through the door that lead straight to the

kitchen, his nose hairs tingled at the smell of food. Peeking on the stove at the covered pots, he wondered what Harlem had cooked up. She had an entire meal laid out that consisted of fried chicken, red beans and rice, cabbage, and cornbread. Enzo's stomach growled as he plucked one of the wings from the pan and tore into it. He finished it off by the time he reached the trash can. Licking his lips, he headed down the hall with the bottle of ginger ale in his hand.

Stepping through the door of his bedroom and seeing Harlem sprawled out across his king size bed had him grinning. Her panties were in her ass, hair in a messy bun and she had one of his tank tops on that was exposing her stomach.

"Damn, she even fine in her sleep," Enzo mumbled, climbing onto the bed.

Running his hands up the back of her thighs, he placed soft, gentle kisses on her ass cheeks. Harlem stirred in her sleep and rolled over. Giving Enzo access to the front of her thighs, he took full advantage of her now facing him and kissed up her thighs. Harlem groaned when he made it to her stomach and stuck his hands underneath her butt. When he ventured further, cupping her breast in one hand while the other lay on her stomach, Enzo frowned and looked down.

"Mmm. Why you stop?" Harlem moaned out sleepily.

Pulling back, Enzo situated himself, so he was sitting on the edge of the bed. "Aye. Sit up real quick."

"Why? I'm sleepy. Just come lay with me."

"Nah. Sit up. I gotta show you something."

Pouting, Harlem yawned and sat up in the bed. Reaching over to the lamp, Enzo flicked it on but didn't make eye contact with her. Wiping the sleep from her eyes, Harlem stared at his back before moving closer. Wrapping her arms around his waist, she inhaled his scent. The Invictus Intense cologne she bought as a just because gift smelled utterly, mouthwatering delicious bouncing off his skin.

"What you need to show me? I hope it's in here," she giggled softly, trying to stick her hands in his pants.

When he grabbed her wrist a little too hard, Harlem sat up in the bed. "W-What's wrong?"

"You pregnant?" he asked evenly.

The question came out more as a statement and had Harlem scooting back some in the bed. Turning around to face her, Enzo stared her in her eyes. When he touched her stomach, it was hard as hell and the way she had been sleeping like crazy, with weird ass mood swings lately explained it all now. She was either pregnant or had some strange shit going on with her body, but Enzo wasn't falling for the latter of the two.

"I-I don't know. I think so," she answered truthfully.

Harlem had saw the change in her body before now. She was just scared to admit it to herself, and to Enzo. Though he seemed genuinely interested in starting a family with her and carrying on their legacy as he put it, Harlem didn't want to get her hopes up high. Reaching across the bed where he placed her ginger ale, he snatched up the pregnancy test and held it out to her.

Tears pooled in Harlem's eyes as she stared at the all too familiar box in his hand. "Y-You want me to take that?" she asked in a shaky breath.

"Yeah. There's only one way to find out, right?"

"I'm scared," she whispered as the tears began to cascade down her cheeks.

Climbing to where she scooted to, Enzo grabbed her hand and looked her in the face. "Ain't no need to be scared. I'm here for you, aight? I ain't going anywhere regardless of what the outcome is."

Sniffling, Harlem wiped her face with the back of her hand. "You promise?"

"I promise, baby."

Enzo was so damn affectionate, it didn't matter how nervous Harlem just was; she wasn't anymore. Helping her up from the bed, the two walked into the bathroom together. Harlem had to pee something serious. Pulling her panties down, she sighed as her bottom touched the cold ceramic seat. Opening the box for her, Enzo held the test out for her to grab.

"You just pee on it, right?" he questioned, flipping the box over to read the instructions.

Harlem nodded her head. "Yes. I pee on it then wait a few minutes for the results."

He nodded as she began to pee. It seemed like forever

when she finally was done. Grabbing some tissue, she placed the test on the counter, wiped herself, pulled up her underwear and washed her hands. Enzo was staring at her through the mirror the entire time. He was nervous too, but he couldn't show it. At least not right now. He knew Harlem needed him if the test came back with the results he had a feeling it would.

"How was your meeting?" She asked, leaning against the sink.

"Productive as hell. I'm ready to get shit moving. You cooked all that food and fell asleep?"

She nodded shyly. "Yes. I couldn't even eat anything when I was done."

Enzo smiled. "Ah yeah? That's the first sign of pregnancy, right?"

She playfully rolled her eyes. "No, it's not."

"Whatever you say, love," he said, raspy voice making Harlem's skin warm all over.

When her eyes glanced in the direction of the test, her skin went cold. Frozen in place, her eyes blinked rapidly at the two pink lines staring back at her as if they were going to jump out. Seeing the expression on her face, Enzo stepped closer, and his chest expanded. Having just read the instructions, he knew exactly what those lines meant. Turning to face him, Harlem was stunned to see tears in his eyes.

"Baby," he choked out, pulling her into his embrace.

Holding her tightly, he nestled his face in the crook of her neck. "You pregnant, ma."

Harlem nodded her head. "Yeah. I guess so."

Enzo lifted up. "You not happy?"

Since they were being honest, Harlem shrugged. "I don't know how to feel honestly, Enzo. I'm scared more than anything, but I just found out, so I may get happy later."

"Damn. Aight. I understand that."

His saddened tone made Harlem grab ahold of his hand. "I'm happy to be sharing this experience with you."

His smile reappeared. "Me too. Now I know why you been acting like that lately. Your hormones are out of fucking whack."

Harlem felt herself about to cry and wiped at her eyes.

"Wait. What you crying for? What I say?" he asked, lost as hell.

"Don't talk to me like that."

Enzo wanted to chuckle, but instead, he pulled her into his chest and kissed the top of her head. "I'm sorry. I'ma try to talk nicer to you, aight?"

"Okay," she mumbled pulling away. "I'll schedule me a doctor's appointment to see how far along I am. What days are you free?"

"Any day you need me to be. It doesn't matter; just know I'ma be there," he said, staring her in the eyes.

This moment was the time Enzo needed to earn her trust back completely. He had been gradually getting it back, but that little hiccup with Chasney had set him back some. This go around, he wasn't taking any chances. He wanted Harlem to understand that he was devoted to only her. His loyalty to her was steadfast. She may not have known it, but Harlem had made him the happiest he had ever been.

The love of his life was carrying his seed. Right there, as they stood toe to toe in his bathroom, Enzo vowed that Harlem was going to be his wife. She was the real definition of ride or die and had long ago earned the place in his heart that no woman could reach. His heart was hers to keep forever. Even if they didn't work out, Enzo couldn't see himself offering his heart to anyone else. Harlem could keep it.

In awe at the figure on the monitor, Harlem snaked her head around to look at Enzo, who shot her a proud grin. On the screen was their baby. A healthy baby who was eight weeks along and giving his mommy the blues already. It'd been a week since they found out she was pregnant, and Harlem had been sick as hell since. She didn't know if it was because of the seasons changing, but she felt miserable. The only reason she even got out of bed today was to check on her baby.

"You still have a way to go, but everything is looking great so far," the doctor affirmed.

"Um, I had a miscarriage some years back. Is there anything I should be concerned about now?" Harlem asked.

She had been wanting to ask a professional in the medical field that question since last week. Instead, Google had been her best friend and worst nightmare. One click on an article about a mother who had over five miscarriages, left her spooked. She was so shaken up; she woke Enzo up. Every night around four in the morning, Harlem was up to use the bathroom and that night was no different. She climbed off the toilet and right into the bed after washing her hands and talked Enzo's ears off until she fell back asleep.

"Nothing to stress over, no. Just be aware of your body and what changes you feel. If at any time you feel lightheaded and dizzy, or you began to bleed out profusely, don't wait to come into emergency. I'll print up your prescription for the nausea you've been experiencing, along with your others. Any questions for me?" Dr. Keith asked.

She was an older black lady in her fifties and had been working at the hospital for over twenty-five years. She saw the questioning gaze in Harlem's eyes and gave her a reassuring smile.

"I think that's all. You have any questions, Enzo?"

"When can we get the ultrasound pictures?" he asked, anxious to see the baby on more than just a monitor. Plus, he couldn't wait to tell his mama. She had been on his ass when he was younger about not knocking a female up, but nowadays he couldn't get her to stop mentioning him giving her some grandbabies. I guess he was of age now, so she was cool with it.

"As early as twelve weeks, but most people get them between eighteen and twenty. It's solely up to you."

Harlem looked over at him and silently they agreed to wait. They were so in tune with one another, they both knew right away what their response would be.

"We'll wait until she's ready then," Enzo replied, blowing Harlem a kiss.

Dr. Keith smiled at the young, in love couple and nodded her head. "Very well then. Ms. Harlem, I'll see you back in here next month."

"Sure thing. Thank you so much," she said appreciative as ever.

"Of course, sweetie. Congratulations again," she said before stepping out the door.

Enzo couldn't wait to pounce on her. Rushing to his feet, he stepped quickly over to where Harlem was sitting on the bed and picked her up.

"Thank you," he beamed, kissing all over her neck.

"You're welcome, silly. Now, stooop," she whined as he began licking down her chest. The v-neck she had on had her cleavage all on display and Enzo wanted to bury his face in her boobs.

"Ain't nobody coming in here. Let me get a taste," he said huskily.

"No, nasty. Wait until we get home."

Surrendering, Enzo smirked as he pulled away but stepped back into her space. Kissing her lips, he palmed her belly. At eight weeks, she wasn't showing at all. Now that he knew she was pregnant though, he couldn't help but notice her small pudge.

"You gone be knocked out when we get home."

"No, I'm not. That's you who be sleeping all day," she laughed as he helped her down from the bed.

Enzo just shrugged. Harlem's pregnancy hormones were rubbing off on Enzo. His appetite had grown tremendously. He was sleeping in later and dozing off during the day; it was so bad. He never took naps during the day before but let Harlem have been snuggled up and getting good sleep in the bed… he was jumping under the covers right with her.

Once they made it to the car, Enzo opened her door and just stood in between her legs with a goofy grin on his face. Harlem smiled back, feeling all mushy inside.

"What, silly?" she asked.

"What you gone do with your other house?"

For a second, Harlem had forgotten all about it. She hadn't been to it in months, but knew it was being cleaned. Dreka had hired a cleaning service to come through every week to keep up the maintenance of it.

"I don't know. Dreka and I went half on it, so I'd have to check with her. Why?"

Enzo scratched at his beard. It was spreading out lovely over his chiseled face, and nasty thoughts of rubbing her pussy all over it invaded Harlem's mind. She smiled as he licked his lips and sighed. *Lord, this man is fine.*

"Was thinking about turning it into a little office space. A few of the rooms at least. You don't need it anymore anyway."

She cocked her head to the side. "And, what makes you think that?"

"Unless you wanna have another body on your hands, *you* better think about why you don't need it. Quit playing with me."

"Awwww," Harlem cooed. "You mad, bae? I was just playing."

"Yeah aight," he mumbled, in his feelings.

He didn't even bother to close her door. Jumping in the driver's seat, Enzo pulled out of the parking lot and ran a list of food spots they could slide through to grab a bite to eat over in his mind. He knew she was hungry 'cause his stomach was touching his damn back. Grabbing his hand, Harlem intertwined her fingers between his, but Enzo didn't do the same. When she sucked her teeth and tried to pull away, he laced his fingers with hers and shot her a smirk that had her panties growing wet.

Placing a kiss to the back of her hand, he said, "You know I got you, right?"

Harlem squeezed his hand tighter, never wanting to let it go. She didn't see how Rose claimed to love Jack and she let her man's hand slip from hers. That bitch was fraud in

Harlem's eyes. Enzo would have been right on her side shivering and all had she starred in the movie.

"Yes. I got you too. For life, Mr. Maverick."

Looking her way, his eyes filled with adoration. He couldn't wait to give her his last name. *Harlem Rayne Maverick*, he said in his head. *Yeah, that got a fucking ring to it. Sound like some boss shit.* He grinned, thinking of ways he could propose. He didn't know when that time would come when he dropped to one knee and asked for her hand in marriage, but he promised to make an honest woman out of Harlem and literally have her back for life.

CHAPTER TEN

"Damn my feet hurt," Andrea grumbled as she and the kids walked in the house.

They headed straight to their rooms and she knew Davion was about to hop right on that game with his little friends.

"Y'all better do that homework before any TV's get turned on," she yelled out, slipping her shoes from her feet.

"Okay!" They shouted back.

Like clockwork, her phone rang, and she pulled it from her purse. Ever since she started working two weeks ago, Harlem would call to check on her. It was more so out of habit and wanting to build their relationship back to where it used to be for Harlem, and Andrea was more than happy to oblige. They had been through the trenches together, and it broke her heart at how distant they'd become over the years.

Andrea felt Harlem just looked at her as a pill-popping junky, and for a while she did. She was also looking for signs of the woman Andrea used to be before Dre. Before the mental, verbal, and physical abuse. Harlem just wanted the strong black woman who raised her to return, and her daily check-ins reassured her that Andrea was almost back to her normal self.

Talking and hanging around Jasmyn put some fire and motivation under Andrea's ass to get her life together. Andrea wasn't envious at all at how Jasmyn's life had turned around for the better while hers took a turn for the worst. Everyone's journey in life isn't the same. What road one person travels down isn't designated for another person. Andrea had to relearn that and accept Jasmyn's amazing support for the friend she was trying to be. She realized that if she didn't heal what hurt her, she'd continue to bleed on the people who loved her when they weren't the ones who had cut her. It was a process, but she was grateful to be back on track with not just her life, but her kid's life as well.

Harlem had suggested rehab, but Andrea declined. She explained to her oldest how she'd been absent long enough in their lives.

"Hey," Andrea answered.

"Hey. Y'all just getting in?" Harlem asked, looking for a movie to watch on Netflix.

Standing to her feet, Andrea headed to the kitchen. "Yes.

I'm wore out, but I'm about to find something for these siblings of yours to eat. What are you doing?"

"In the bed looking for a movie to watch."

Andrea pulled her phone away from her ear and looked at the time. "It's only six-forty-seven. The sun is still out," she said with a chuckle.

"I know. But it's dark in here thanks to my blackout curtains."

"Hmm. I guess. Where's Enzo? How are y'all doing?"

Harlem smiled and glanced her man's way. He was in the middle of texting Meechi about a business venture but stop typing when he felt Harlem's eyes on him. Leaning her way, he pecked her cheek and rubbed her belly.

She had just reached her four month mark a few days ago and her belly was finally starting to poke out. Enzo couldn't keep his hands off her. That was the reason they were in bed now. Having sex, sleeping, and eating was all the couple seemed to do. Harlem was happy she didn't have a job or her ass would have been fired.

"We're good. He's right here."

"What up, Ms. Andrea," Enzo spoke.

"Tell him I said hi."

Harlem did then thought about how she was going to tell her mama she was pregnant. Though she wasn't showing drastically, she didn't know how she'd look in a few weeks and not visiting wasn't an option. Bree made sure of that.

"We should all have dinner together soon," she suggested, and Enzo smirked, knowing exactly what she was up to.

Andrea smiled wide. "I'd love that, baby. When were you thinking so I can go grocery shopping?"

"Um, it'll be a few other people coming too. Is that okay?"

"Who are they first? I don't want everyone up and through my place," Andrea said, sounding just like she did when Harlem was a teenager and stayed trying to have Yaz and Sarena over.

Chuckling she said, "Just Enzo's cousin, Dreka and Yaz."

"Oh okay. Not too many people. I'll invite my homegirl since her son is coming."

"Oh goodness," Harlem laughed just as her lined clicked.

Pulling the phone away from her ear, she frowned when she saw Lucci's name pop up on her screen. Enzo peeked at her screen once she turned it his way and told her to answer it.

"Ma, I'ma talk to you later."

"Okay. Love you."

"Love you too," she replied before clicking over and was met with Lucci hollering loudly in her ear.

On the other side of town, Lucci had just gotten busted. Well, in Yaz' eyes, he was busted. After not answering her phone calls after she called him three times, Yaz contemplated on popping up at his crib. The contemplation only lasted a few seconds because she was already in her car and backing out of her driveway once she made her decision. Being ignored was the quickest way to piss her off.

For just some dude she was getting money out of, she didn't care about being ignored. Lucci ignoring her though? Oh, no. That wasn't about to fly. He wasn't a regular nigga to her anymore and hadn't been for a while. Why he wanted to play games with her, Yaz wasn't sure, but she was about to show him just how much fun playing games with her was. She always won.

"Aye! Come get this girl, man," Lucci let out in a chuckle, running around his car.

With a BB gun aimed his way, Yaz pulled the trigger and sent a metal bullet straight to his calf muscle. Pulling it again, she connected with his arm that he was trying to hold his leg with and grinned.

"Ahhh! Fuck!" Lucci screamed loudly.

The female he walked out of the house with was ducking down on the porch, but if Yaz really wanted to pop her ass, she could have. This wasn't about her though. She didn't give a fuck about the scantily clad woman; she was there for Lucci. When she pulled up to the house, she saw an unfamiliar car that was much too girly for any of his niggas to be pushing, parked on the curb. Instead of walking to the door and knocking like a normal person, Yaz waited in her car for them to come outside. Never in a million years did she think she'd do some crazy shit like this, but there came a time for everything.

"Just tell me why you were ignoring me, and I won't shoot you again," she said calmly.

"Man, nah! Fuck outta here. I should smack the fuck outta you. Look at my leg!" he roared.

Harlem had placed him on speaker and she and Enzo couldn't help but laugh. If he thought calling Harlem was going to save him, he was sadly mistaken.

"Nigga, don't call my girl 'cause you on some bullshit. We chilling. Keep all that drama ova there," Enzo said into the phone.

"Aight. Remember that hoe ass nigga," Lucci hissed, hanging up and sliding the phone in the pocket of his shorts. The shorts he had no underwear on underneath. His big dick was swinging everywhere and pissing Yaz off even more. That let her know he and scary cat on the porch had been doing more than just talking like he claimed.

"You out here with your dick all out. I should shoot that muthafucka," she snarled, making Lucci cover his dick up with both hands.

"Yo! Chill out!" He yelled.

"Oh my gosh. Please don't do that," the girl cried.

Yaz cut her eyes in her direction and mugged her something vicious.

"Hoe, why is you even still here? I ain't worried about you. Climb up off my nigga's porch and stop worrying about the dick you ain't gon' ever get again."

Slowly, the girl lifted up and on trembling legs walked off

the porch. When she was almost past Yaz, Yaz pointed the BB gun at her, and she took off running to her car. Lucci would have laughed at the way she almost busted her ass getting to her car, but he took that opportunity to rush Yaz while her eyes weren't on him. With the speed of a cheetah, he tackled her against the driver's side of his car and squeezed her wrist, so she'd let the gun go.

"Get off me!" Yaz hissed.

"Let this muthafucka go before you hurt yourself!"

"No!"

Biting down hard on her neck, Yaz' grip loosened up, and Lucci snatched the gun out of her hand, dropping it into the pocket of his shorts. Grabbing her arms, he placed them above her head as they both breathed hard as hell in one another's face.

"I can't stand your black ass," Yaz fussed, clenched her teeth.

"Shut yo' crazy ass up. This the shit I gotta deal with when it comes to you? Huh? Shooting fucking BB guns at me and shit. Got my skin burning."

"So? That's what your ass gets. You'll know next time not to ignore me. Over here laid up with some prostitute."

Lucci sucked his teeth. "She wasn't a prostitute with your silly ass."

"Looked like it to me. I ain't know that's what you were in to. Jail got you out here getting any type of pussy, huh? I wonder what you were in there doing," she said, smirking.

Slamming her body against the car forcefully, Lucci backed away from her. "You got me fucked up. Ole bobble-head ass. Head too big for your fucking body," he joked.

"Whatever. Give me my shit back so I can leave."

"You ain't getting shit back. This mine now, ma. Shoulda thought about that before you pulled up over here," he said, walking away from her to go in the house.

Running behind him, Yaz jumped on his back, trying to pull him down. Successful with catching him off guard, the two fell into the lawn, and she locked her legs around his waist, and arms around his neck.

"Stupid ass," she laughed as they rolled around.

"Get off me, man. Gon' have all these bugs in my hair and shit."

Yaz slapped him upside the head. "Fuck your hair. I put these braids in there anyway."

Lucci couldn't do anything but lay there, laugh and shake his head. Yaz was a different breed for sure. She was playful, drop-dead gorgeous, with a personality that Lucci couldn't even be mad at. He really fucked with her the long way, but his hoe-ish ways were hard to let go.

"Yo. You really wildin' out. Can we just go in the house?"

"Nope," Yaz said, letting him loose and standing up. "I'm going home."

Standing to his feet, Lucci brushed the grass off his arms and legs. "You came all the way over here, showed your ass and about to leave?"

"Yep. Right after you go in the house and grab me some gas money. I'm good now."

He sucked his teeth and twisted his lips to the side ready to call her bluff. "You good now? So, you ain't mad?"

Yaz smiled. "Nope. I'm not mad at all. Today showed me exactly what type of nigga I'm dealing with."

"You been knew what type of nigga you was dealing with, though. So, what you getting at? I ain't with all the riddles."

"You're a hoe. I specifically told you what this," she said, pointing between them, "was. Yet, you wanted to play with me so I'ma just do me."

"Here your dramatic ass go," Lucci huffed, stepping out of the grass and sitting on the porch steps. When he thought about Yaz swinging on him while she was standing up, he stood to his feet.

"Yeah," she huffed, reaching out and grabbing his dick. "Here I go. Got your dick all out just like a hoe."

Laughing, Lucci slapped her hand away. "Watch out, man."

"I'ma watch out alright."

"You so dramatic. That girl ain't mean shit to me. Let's go inside."

Yaz shot him a look of disgust. "Absolutely not. She ain't mean shit, but you had her in your crib? When you start being loose like that?"

Shaking his head, Lucci ran a hand down his face. The only reason Shatira was still at his crib when Yaz pulled up was because she claimed she had to use the restroom. Her car wouldn't start after she brought Lucci some food, and they had to go buy a new battery for it. On their way back, they got pulled over, and Shatira tucked the weed Lucci had on him after he tossed it in her lap. She didn't even ask any questions. She was willing to catch a case behind his ass.

Thankfully, the cop that pulled him over wasn't on any bullshit and let them go after claiming he thought he saw Lucci make an illegal U-turn. Truth was, he did make an illegal U-turn, but once he saw who was in the driver's seat, the cop let him go. It was crazy the amount of fear he put in some cops. Had it been another who had it out for him, he'd be getting bonded out right now instead of having this conversation with Yaz.

Grateful for her willingness to look out for him, Lucci let Shatira suck him off before sending her on her way. He wasn't purposely trying to ignore Yaz, but he didn't want to be rude. Shorty had come through in the clutch and he just wanted to show his appreciation by sticking his dick down her throat. He didn't see what the problem was.

"Bruh," Lucci stressed. "All she did was suck me off. Goddamn. You trippin' like we-"

"Like we what? Go together?" She chuckled. "Nah. I'm tripping like you aren't the one who said you like your bitches crazy. Well, look what you got!" she said, throwing her arms in the air. "Blame yourself. The next time that phone ring and you ignore me, remember this day."

"I ain't fucking with you no more, man," Lucci laughed, eyeing her frame.

She was rocking her work attire. Casual ankle length dress pants, a cute BeBe pleated top and Chanel sandals. Her hips were poking out, making Lucci lick his lips as he imagined hitting her from the back while he pulled on her long, blonde braids. The bright color against her dark skin was making his dark hard. She looked sexy as fuck standing there looking like his little African princess.

"Bet. Keep that same energy when I do me. I won't pop up on you and you won't pop up on me."

"I ain't say all that silly shit," he grimaced while she hit him with a smirk.

"Nope. That's exactly what you said."

With that being said, Yaz turned around and walked toward her car. She knew she wasn't going to get her gun back, so she didn't even bother trying to. Instead, she just hopped in her car, hit the locks and pulled her phone out. Going to her Cash App, she requested five hundred dollars from $*LucciBaby*, and put 'Wasting My Time' in the *for* section. Lucci was about to knock on her window and see why her ass was still sitting there until his phone vibrated.

Pulling it out his pocket, he chuckled at the request she sent him. When Yaz' phone vibrated stating he paid her, she grinned, honked her horn as a thank you, and backed out of his driveway. Lucci stood with a silly grin on his face watching her car peel off down the road. He may have been fussing about her crazy antics, but deep down, he was with all that crazy shit. He just hoped Yaz kept that same energy when she did some shaky shit because he knew that day was coming. Women like Yaz didn't play fair at all, and she surely wasn't after today's festivities.

Harlem couldn't stop wringing her hands together. Finally, the day had come for the big dinner at her mama's house, and she was a nervous wreck. The slightly oversized black button-down t-shirt dress she was wearing didn't make her feel any less pregnant. Her stomach had grown to a size anyone could spot out with a fitted t-shirt on and she hated wearing jeans now. Her body was transforming right before her eyes and she couldn't believe it. Though she was comfortable in the cotton material, her nerves were shot.

"Relax, ma," Enzo chuckled, shooting her a soothing smile. His raspy voice somewhat calming her nerves.

Harlem released a shaky breath as she stared at the side of his face. Enzo was looking mighty fine today, as he did all other days, but today Harlem was seeing him in a different light. She didn't know if it was because he had been so supportive since finding out she was pregnant or what, but just looking at him had her hot and bothered.

His muscular arms flexed with the slightest motion of him gripping the steering wheel. Every time he moved, the scent of his intoxicating cologne invaded Harlem's nose. She was lost in a trance, captivated by the veins in his hands, tattoos covering his arms and neck, and thick, juicy lips. Feeling her gaze on him, Enzo looked her way as they came to a red light.

"You horny?" he asked with a hint of humor laced through his words.

Breathing hard, Harlem nodded her head. "You look and smell so good," she purred, grabbing ahold of his hand.

Placing his hand between her legs, Harlem licked her luscious lips at the warmth that radiated through her body from his touch. Enzo didn't know when she unbuttoned the last couple of buttons on her shirt, but he wasn't complaining at all. Leaning her seat back, Harlem spread her legs and was thankful as ever for whoever created tint for windows.

Pulling her panties to the side, Enzo dipped his fingers inside her gushiness and had to get a sample before getting her off. Sticking his fingers in his mouth, sucking her juices clean, he chuckled when Harlem moaned. With his hand now back between her legs, Enzo toyed with her clit as he drove to her mama's house. Harlem's breathing began to accelerate as her orgasm snuck up on her quicker than she expected it to.

"Oooh, Enzo," she moaned softly, making his dick harder than what it already was.

"That's it," he coached. "Get that nut off so you can relax, baby."

Rubbing her clit faster, he felt himself begin to speed as

Harlem gripped his wrist and rotated her hips. He damn near swerved off the road when he glanced her way. Her head was tilted back, mouth slightly ajar, and face a flustered mess. Her fuck faces had him ready to pull over.

"Aaaah, shit," she cried, as her legs shook and the grip on his wrist tightened.

Enzo didn't pull his hand away until they were in her mama's driveway. Breathing hard, Harlem licked her lips and smiled a content smile. Fixing her panties, Enzo slid his fingers in her mouth and looked on as she nastily twirled her tongue, collecting the mess she made from his fingers.

"That's why you're carrying my child now. Little freaky ass," he jested, with a smirk. "Now, I'ma have to walk in here and shake your mama's hand with pussy juice on my fingers."

Laughing, Harlem buttoned her dress up. "You better not."

"You good now?" he asked, admiring her beauty.

In his eyes, she was even more beautiful. Her glow was different and not just because she was pregnant. It was a happy glow. One that'd been hiding in the dark for so long, Enzo just had to take a minute and appreciate it. Had this been another time, and not one he knew was important to her, he'd make her sit on his dick right then and there and make love to her. Now wasn't the time, but when they got home? He was putting in work.

"Yes. Great actually," she giggled, and leaned over to kiss

his lips. Running her hand through his beard, she sucked on his bottom lip and moaned before pulling away.

"Aight. Bring your ass on before I have you squirting all over these leather seats," he growled.

"Ooh! Don't threaten me with a good time," she laughed.

Walking to the door, Enzo had to get a feel of her belly before they got inside. As soon as his hand touched her belly, Harlem felt a small kick. Eyes wide, they shot up to Enzo who had a look of confusion on his face.

"What?"

"T-The baby just kicked me," she said in utter surprise.

"For real," Enzo said excitedly, now rubbing his hand all over her belly, so he could feel the baby kick as well.

"It was small but – oh!" she squealed, when it happened again. This time, Enzo's hand was directly where the kick was delivered.

His heart expanded in his chest as he and Harlem stared at one another. "You really pregnant, baby," he beamed, as if she wasn't five months. She was indeed pregnant for real. Not for play.

"I am," she chuckled, just as the door opened.

Though he didn't want to, Enzo pulled his hands away from her abdomen and placed one at her waist.

"Sissy!" Bree squealed, throwing herself into Harlem and hugging her tightly.

"Hey boo. You must miss me," Harlem laughed as they stepped inside.

"I always miss you. You look pretty."

Harlem grinned. "Thank you. So do you."

"What up, Bree," Enzo spoke.

Giving him a hug as well, she said, "Hi, Enzo. You talked her into this, huh?"

"I didn't know anything about it until today," he fibbed, receiving Bree's squinted eyes as if she were reading through his lie.

"Mhm. Well, mama is in the kitchen and Yaz and some guy are here, but they're acting weird," she explained with her face scrunched up.

Harlem chuckled. She knew she could only be talking about her friend and Lucci's dysfunctional asses. While Bree showed Enzo where the guest bathroom was around the corner, Harlem walked into the kitchen, and her stomach growled. Andrea had it smelling better than good in there, and she couldn't wait to eat.

"Hey, mama," she spoke, walking up on her.

Andrea's face lit up. "Hey. Look at you looking all fly."

Peeping her daughters' attire, Andrea wondered how she could get that dress from her. Or, at least get the details of where she got it from.

"Thank you. I like your hair."

"I tried to do a little something different. It's okay?"

Harlem nodded. She loved the burgundy color she had added to her dark brown hair. It looked good against her brown skin. Peeking at the stove, Harlem licked her lips and rubbed her hands together.

"Yes. It fits you. Where's Ms. Jasmyn?"

"Girl, if you don't just call me Jasmyn, I know something," she said, walking into the kitchen. In her hand was a bottle of wine and in the other was her purse.

Smiling, Harlem shook her head. "If you say so. How are you?"

"I'm not even going to lie, sweetie. I was just pissed off about twenty minutes ago, but I'm good now," she replied.

"Why? What happened?" Andrea questioned.

"Girl, Eli and Enzo's nappy headed ass daddy. He knew it was his weekend to keep him but tried to get amnesia when it was time for me to leave. Talking about some 'Damn. I'ma be busy this weekend.' Like I don't be busy every day, but do I complain? Hell, no. I do what a mother is supposed to do. We got to arguing and shit, and I just hung up in his face. He pulled up fifteen minutes later trying to apologize. I told his black ass to kiss my ass."

Laughing, Andrea said, "And he probably would have if you let him."

"So, his wife can try to trip on me over him coming at me? Chile, please. I don't have the time."

"What you in hear fussin' about already?" Enzo asked, stepping into the kitchen.

Hitting the women with his handsome grin, they all smiled up at him since he was towering over their frames.

Hugging his mama, he placed a kiss on her cheek. Harlem didn't peep the orange Hermès shopping bag in his hand until he was handing it to Andrea.

"How you doing, Ms. Andrea? Harlem and I got you a little something for cooking all this food," he said smoothly.

Andrea looked puzzled as if she didn't want to take it from his hand.

"If you don't grab it, I surely will," Yaz said as she walked into the kitchen. Bree had caught her coming from the bathroom and talked her ear off until Yaz told her it was time to eat.

Chuckling nervously, Andrea grabbed the bag. Pulling the purse out of the dust bag it was in, her eyes widened at the beautiful rose Jaipur color.

"Wow. This is gorgeous. Thank you both," she said humbly.

Though the gift was strictly from Enzo, he included Harlem in on it as well. They were a team now, so all gifts from here on out were from them together unless stated otherwise. After Harlem explained to Enzo how proud of her she was, Enzo thought it'd be nice to get her something for pushing through her battle. The gesture was simple, but it almost brought Andrea to tears. She was grateful for the simple things in life like Harlem and her talking on the phone, so a five thousand dollar bag had her elated.

"You're welcome. Now you can get rid of your other purse," Harlem suggested.

"Yes. Give it to your sister since she keeps asking for it."

It was a Coach purse, but Bree didn't care what the brand was. She just wanted another purse to add to her collection. Hearing that, the wheels in Enzo's head began to turn. Harlem glanced his way and shook her head, already knowing he was about to spoil Bree more than she already was.

"I'ma hook Bree up too, then," Enzo voiced.

"Shit. Hook me up. You passing out bags," Jasmyn added with a chuckle. "That's fly, girl."

"Thank you. Let me go put this in my room and we can eat."

Everyone said okay or nodded in agreement, as she walked away to her room. Lucci walked in from outside after taking a phone call from Deuce and looked Yaz up and down. Neither of them had spoken a word to one another, and Lucci was two seconds away from yoking her ass up. But, he was only going to chill because this wasn't his shit to be acting a fool in. He would if Yaz made him though.

"What up, fam," he said, as he and Enzo slapped hands before embracing one another in a hug.

"Not a thing. Y'all rode together?"

"No," Yaz spat a little too harshly for Lucci's liking.

"Aye. Don't say it like you too good to ride in my shit. You was just trying to suck me off in that bitch not too long ago," he said, whispering loud enough for Harlem and Enzo to hear. Jasmyn had gone to sit down at the table across the room far out of ear reach.

Yaz pushed him away from her and rolled her eyes. After the incident with Shatira, the two got back cool, but they were at odds this time because of Yaz. They went to the club together the other night and were rolling hard off a pill. Ready to fuck until it wore off, they dipped off to Yaz' crib at four in the morning. On the way there, Yaz' tried her hardest to suck his dick while he drove, but Lucci was too fucked up. If that was going to be her first time sucking him off, he didn't want it in the car. When they got inside, Yaz had forgotten all about the hoodie lying across her bed.

It belonged to a guy named DeKhari she called herself messing around with. She pulled up on him earlier that day and hopped in his car, so they could just talk and chill. It started raining, and he offered her his hoodie. She promised to give it back to him the next time she saw him, but that wouldn't be happening. Giving his hoodie back that is. Once Lucci peeped the smell of cologne and realized it wasn't hers, he went straight to her kitchen, grabbed some scissors and cut that bitch up. Afterward, he fucked her against the kitchen counter before leaving her right there with a wet ass while sprinkling the shreds of the hoodie over her head like the asshole he was. That was over a week ago, and Lucci was still mad about the situation.

"Yeah, yeah," Yaz said, waving him off. "Like I said. No. We didn't ride here together. I got moves to make after this."

"You really gone make me fuck you up, bruh. On everything I love," Lucci hissed.

"Everything? That's a little extreme for someone you claim to not fuck with," Yaz said sarcastically.

"Y'all are not about to irritate me with this bullshit," Harlem said, making Enzo chuckle lowly under his breath. "I'm too damn hungry and y'all too old."

Harlem walked away, while Lucci and Yaz both looked at Enzo with questioning eyes. He knew his baby was just hungry, so he just hit them with a shoulder shrug.

"Aye. She got a point.," he chuckled, following behind Harlem.

Thirty minutes later, everyone sat around the table, laughing and eating. Dreka had shown up right when they were about to say prayer. Harlem's stomach fluttered as she prepared to tell everyone why they were really all sitting around her mama's table as if it were Thanksgiving.

"Harlem. Gone head and finish that bottle of wine off, girl," Jasmyn encouraged.

Nervously, Harlem let out a chuckle just as Enzo gave her thigh a reassuring squeeze. It was now or never.

"I'm okay. I can't drink for a while."

"Why? You on antibiotics?" Andrea questioned.

Harlem felt like she wanted to throw up. Andrea was asking a logical question, but it reminded Harlem of when she got caught stealing at the mall and had to call her to pick her up. Though she was grown and had been providing for herself for a while now, revealing this news to her mama was hard.

"No. I-I'm, uh. We're having a baby," she said quietly.

The entire table quieted. Andrea blinked her eyes in sheer surprise. Jasmyn's mouth was wide open, and Yaz had tears in her eyes. Dreka was just smiling. She knew something was up with her girl the way she had been missing in action lately.

"Oh my gosh!" Yaz squealed, beyond happy for her friend.

"Are you serious?" Andrea said, getting emotional.

Nodding, Harlem sniffled as her emotions got the best of her. "Yes. I'm five months along."

"Thank the Lord," Jasmyn praised, making Harlem chuckle.

"You knew, mama?" Enzo asked.

"Not at all, but I'm not surprised. All you ever talk about is Harlem this, Harlem that," she joked, making the table erupt in laughter. Enzo had it bad.

"It's okay, baby. They're some haters," Harlem told him, turning his way. He pecked her lips and grinned.

"I know they are."

"I'm just trying to figure out why I wasn't told about this before everyone else? I ain't like these common folks; me and my little cuz gon' have a special bond."

"The only one special in the equation is you. I always

knew you were a little slow growing up," Jasmyn joked, making Yaz laugh hard.

"Aight. Laugh all y'all want to. Watch when he get here how close we be," Lucci replied.

"He!" the table all but yelled.

Harlem shook her head. "No. We don't know what we're having yet."

"Well, congratulations anyway, baby. I-I'm so happy," Andrea said, now choked up even more.

Standing to her feet, Harlem walked around to her and they hugged. When they pulled away, Harlem grabbed her hand and placed it on her belly. Andrea's eyes widened.

"You're hiding all that stomach under this dress. I should have known something was up," Andrea chuckled.

"Can I touch?" Bree asked.

Nodding with a smile, Harlem grabbed her little sister's hand and placed it on her belly.

"Whoa! It's so hard," she exclaimed.

"I know. It's a baby in there. Your niece or nephew."

"Bruh. You are not grown," Davion spat, making Harlem look his way.

"You on the hater team today too?"

Davion shot her a smile and shook his head. "Nah. I'm just weirded out, man. I know what you gotta do to have a baby."

"Yep. Kissing gets a girl pregnant, so you better keep your lips to yourself," Yaz told him.

"Nah. That ain't what I lear–"

"Okaaay," Harlem dragged. "Enough of that. I've been holding that in for a while now. I wanted all the people I love to be in one room while we shared this exciting news."

"Well, I'm happy for you both. I know you'll be an amazing mother because you've had the perfect example," Jasmyn said, smiling Harlem's way though she complimented Andrea.

Smiling, Andrea chimed in. "And, he or she will have a standup dad. Enzo, you better take care of my baby. Both of them," she warned.

"Of course. That was the plan since we met," he replied with ease, making Harlem fall deeper in love. "She and my seed are good for life. Bree too," he said, giving Bree a wink.

"Man," Lucci let out. "Wait until you tell auntie. She gon' be expecting me to pop out with one next. I ain't for all that, but I'm happy for y'all, man. Harlem, you been sis-in-law since day one since me and Enzo are practically brothers. Don't expect a nigga to babysit until he like three, though. And can use the bathroom without me having to change a diaper."

"We shouldn't have told him," Harlem whispered to Enzo but loud enough for Lucci to hear.

He waved them off. "Whatever. I'm just telling y'all what it is now."

"I'll happily babysit, boo," Dreka said. "I miss when mine couldn't talk back," she chuckled.

"Thank you. Whew," she laughed, sitting back down. "Now I can really go in on my plate."

Leaning over, Enzo kissed her cheek and rubbed her thigh underneath the table. "Proud of you, shorty. That wasn't so bad, was it?"

"Thanks to you, it sure wasn't," she said, reminding him of the release he gave her in the car.

Enzo smooched her lips and grinned. As happy as he was right now, Harlem could ask him to hit another lick and he'd be all down for it if that's what she wanted. Their last heist on Trill had set them up beyond lovely. So much so, that Harlem really didn't have to work another day in her life if she didn't want to, but she still would. The break she was on was lovely, no doubt, but the hustler in her wasn't just going to chill. She now had a child to take care of, and though money wasn't everything, it sure did change her life for the better. The only struggle she wanted her child to know about was the one she went through

Later on that evening, after a much needed nap, Enzo was crawling in between Harlem's legs as promised. He woke up having to piss something terrible, and when he came back out, Harlem had stretched her tiny frame all over his side. She slept wild as shit, but Enzo didn't mind. Licking his lips, he admired her silhouette in the dark.

Her belly was on display thanks to the half t-shirt she slipped on before climbing in bed. Ever since she got pregnant, she hated sleeping under the cover as well. The sheet was at her waist, and in seconds being lifted upward as Enzo climbed underneath it. Spreading her legs, he peeled her panties off and gently caressed her thighs before he dived in head first.

"Mmm," Harlem moaned out, grabbing the back of his head, wanting to keep him there forever.

Easing his hand up her shirt, Enzo gripped her breast and continued sucking on her clit. Harlem's legs twitched when he toyed with her right nipple and then the left one. Seeing her reaction to that, Enzo made his way to her nipples and showed them both equal love as he swirled them around on his mouth. They had been her sensitive spot recently, and Harlem felt herself about to come already.

"Oh shit, baaae," she cried. "I'm 'bout to cum."

"Don't cum yet," he demanded, while snatching his boxers down.

Lifting her left leg up, Enzo slid into her and released a throaty groan. She was so tight and so wet, he knew for a fact he wasn't going to last long. He felt like he was backstroking in the pussy she was leaking so much. Harlem was in a state of bliss as Enzo made love to her body. Kissing all over her neck, then moving to her lips that were in a pout, he sucked on her tongue as her muscles flexed around his pole.

"Damn, this pussy is so good," he panted, lifting up and rolling over onto his back. "Get on top, baby."

Oh. He wanna have sex sex, Harlem thought, licking her lips. Straddling his lap, she grabbed his dick and slowly slid down onto him. Immediately, she felt him all in her stomach. How his dick was this good was still a mystery to her, but she wasn't going to complain at all.

"You so damn fine," Enzo grinned, rubbing all over her belly while she swirled her hips.

Running her fingers through her hair, she leaned forward and pecked his lips, lifting her hips up and down in the process. Enzo felt her juices sliding down his pole and onto his thighs. Gripping her around the waist, he slapped her ass hard before giving it a soothing rub.

"Oooh! I love you," Harlem breathed out heavily. "I love you so much."

"I love your ass too."

Buried deep inside her guts, Enzo made sure to bring her to her peak before he released inside her. Had she not already been pregnant, that nut right there would have done the trick. Lying flat on his chest, Harlem placed sensual, juicy kisses along his jawline while he rubbed her booty. That quickly, she was about to fall asleep but then thought of something.

"Enzo," she called out.

"Huh?"

"You never apologized for shooting me."

The rumble from his laughter had Harlem's body bouncing atop his. Enzo smacked her booty as she sat up and glared down at him.

"I'm serious," she stated.

"I know. That's why I'm laughing. You want me to say

sorry for making you jump in front of the gun?" he asked sarcastically.

"Yep. Sure do."

"Aight. My fault."

Sucking her teeth, Harlem tried climbing off him. Laughing, Enzo quickly pulled her down onto his chest. The feeling of her growing belly against his abs was one he had grown to love.

"You play too much," she fussed.

Kissing her shoulder where her scar was, Enzo rubbed her back and said, "I'm sorry, though it wasn't my fault. You shoulda let me off that bitch when she had you running through Briscoe's crib on some flunky shit. Bet yo' ass know better now," he scolded as the first image of seeing Harlem in over five years clouded his mind.

Even with her being an intruder at the time, he had to admit that she was sexy as hell all masked up. He gladly took partial responsibility for her hitting licks, but that part of their life was over with. This past year had showed him just how real karma was. He didn't want any more bad shit happening to either one of them so, it was best to lay their scamming ways to rest.

"I really do now. Can you go get me a bowl of watermelon?" she asked, yawning all in his face.

"Nah. It's too late for the sweet shit."

"Enzooo. Stop playing with me. Come on. I just want a little bit," she whined.

Sitting up with her warm pussy still clamped down on his dick that was hard again, he smirked before kissing her lips a few times. She stared into his mesmerizing honey-colored eyes giving him her best puppy dog expression.

"Aight. But you coming down there with me. I'ma heat up them leftovers," he said, and she nodded.

"Okay," she replied, climbing off his lap.

Enzo's eyes roamed her thick, golden brown frame as she stared down at their juices sliding down her legs. He was absolutely smitten with his best friend, turned lover, enemy, then lover again.

"I can get used to this domestic shit," he said out the blue.

"Oh yeah? You buying us a new crib, is that what you're saying?"

Chuckling, he swung his legs around planting his feet on the ground. "I will. Only once you finish school."

"How about just one year first? I am about to have your child," she said, rubbing her belly.

"One year of school with straight A's, and you got a new crib."

Harlem smiled widely. "See. That's why I fucks with you."

Chuckling, Enzo stood to his feet and pulled her into a hug. "You ain't really ever had a choice but to, shorty. Know that."

He sealed his words with a kiss to her nose, making Harlem blush even harder. For once in her chaotic life,

Harlem was at peace. Her relationship with her mom was back on track. She was setting forth to accomplish past goals, had a man who loved her beyond her wildest dreams, and was carrying their child, who in a way was a product of their environment. Had neither of their parent's gone to shelter that dreadful day years ago, Harlem honestly didn't know where she would be in life.

Right here in this moment, with Enzo by her side, is where she'd prefer to stay though. They had come such a long way from the gutta and had no intentions of ever going back.

"Hoe, you really are pregnant!" Yaz yelled into the phone, making Harlem chuckle with a roll of her eyes.

"See. That's why I don't let you see me. You too fucking dramatic for me."

They were on FaceTime while she waited for Enzo to come out of the property he was viewing for his new business. Opening a hookah bar was never in the plans. For as long as he could remember, he just wanted to rob niggas. The adrenaline rush he received from running through niggas' cribs was one nothing could compare to. That was because he had nothing better to compare it to until now.

Wanting to be a better man for not just himself, but Harlem as well, Enzo knew far before they found out she was pregnant that he needed to change his life around before he ended up in jail or dead. He promised to never leave Harlem's side again, and he meant that shit.

"Girl, what the hell ever. That belly is sticking out too far," she laughed. "You sure you're not carrying twins?"

"I'll slap Enzo if I am. This little boy already has me uncomfortable as hell. I can't imagine what two of him would feel like," Harlem huffed.

"He think it's a girl still, huh?"

Harlem smirked. "Yep. And won't let me tell him otherwise."

After finding out what she was having, Enzo told her not to tell him. Whatever the gender, he was going to be happy with, but since being around Bree and spoiling her like she was his, Enzo made up in his mind that Harlem was having a girl. In his mind, it was only right since he had been practicing with how to deal with them for a while now.

"Y'all are so cute. It's almost sickening," Yaz fake gagged.

"Thanks, hoe. What's up with you and my boy Lucci?"

"Who?"

Harlem laughed. "You know who I'm talking about."

"Girl, fuck him for real."

"Yeah, that's what you need to be doing instead of running your mouth. Come wrap them lips around this dick since you wanna talk so much," Lucci hissed, walking into Yaz' room. Every day she regretting giving his ass a key to her crib.

Laughing, Harlem shook her head. "Oh. You sucking dick now?"

Yaz hollered. "Fuck you too! I ain't putting my mouth on shit. He better go back to where he came from. Walking in here with them raggedy ass braids in his head. Got me fucked up."

Snatching the phone out her hand, Lucci mushed her head. "What up, sis? How the baby doing?"

"Fine. You better stop playing with my friend."

"She like playing games, you ain't know? Nah, you know. You used to be on the same shit."

"Give me my phone back," Yaz yelled, kicking him hard in the back of his knee, making him buckle at the legs.

Caught off guard, Lucci stumbled with a chuckle. "You'll be mad if I throw this bitch down the steps."

"Why would you do that ignorant shit?" Yaz hissed.

"Welp. That's my cue to go," Harlem chuckled just as her baby kicked.

It felt like he was really in there doing backflips honestly. As soon as she hung up, Enzo was opening the driver's side door and climbing in. Harlem was only in the car because she had horrible gas and didn't want to embarrass them for stinking up the place. She let her eyes roam his body as if she hadn't been in his presence all day. It was cold out now, and his fly business attire had Harlem ready to climb over in his lap.

He looked dapper as ever in a black trench coat, nice

black slacks, crisp button-down and black skully cap pulled over his head. When he took it off and rubbed a hand down his waves, Harlem's nipples hardened. Shaking her head at how horny she was, she looked away, but Enzo had already caught her lustful eyes.

"You good over there?" He chuckled as she rubbed her belly.

"Yes. Your child is just having a fucking blast in there. Like, what is he doing," she groaned.

Enzo drew his head back. "He?"

Harlem tucked her lips into her mouth as her eyes slowly skirted his way. "What?"

"You said *he*, as in my son?" he asked, now grinning.

"I said that? I think you're making stuff up."

"Nah," he laughed, leaning her way. Placing his hands on her belly that was sitting comfortably in a Gucci Bee sweater, Enzo's eyes lit up when their son began to move around at his touch. He was always eager to feel the baby move, but an unexplainable feeling came over him knowing she was carrying his junior. When he began to speak, Harlem's entire body melted at the raw emotion in his voice.

"What up, my boy. I see you giving your mama a hard time, but ease up, aight? She loves you and you're a product of me, so you gotta act right. I love everything about you already, though I thought you were a girl," he chuckled and continued. "I already know you're about to change my life and make me an even better man, so just chill out in there, and when you get here, I'll show you what life is really like. Give you and your mama the world, you hear me? I got y'all for life."

Harlem had tears running down her face when he lifted up. Wiping them away, Enzo kissed her lips repeatedly until she was tonguing him down. Enzo showing that much vulnerability toward their child had Harlem's heart in shambles. At almost seven months pregnant, her experience with carrying a child has been one she prayed for. She didn't know if God was listening, considering the sins she committed throughout her life, but she prayed for Enzo and their child to have a relationship that was nothing like she and her dad's.

She knew Enzo wasn't going anywhere, but him having that bonding moment with his son was the security confirmation she didn't know she needed until now. When they broke away from their intense kiss, leaving them both breathless, Enzo smirked and sat back in his seat.

"I'm having a boy," he said to himself, lowly at first before shouting it aloud. "I'm having a fucking boooy!"

Harlem chuckled and grabbed his hand, placing it back on her belly. Baby boy was in there celebrating with him, too. The smile in his eyes and on his face was something no one could take away from him. They'd have to put up a fight with Enzo before he let a muthafucka come between his happiness. And, you better believe Harlem was going to be right there with him fighting too.

EPILOGUE

Sitting in front of a circle of teenaged girls, Harlem gave them all a soft smile as she let her words sink in. Speaking to the group every other week was something she found herself enjoying more than she imagined. What started out as a volunteer position, turned into a job. She didn't look at it as a job, even though she got paid.

Being a domestic violence youth advocate at a local shelter in her city was a reminder of how far she and her family had come. Witnessing survivors come into shelter every day and strive to get their life back on track was what she loved. Not everyone was on the same path though. Especially a few of the teenagers in her group.

"I want you ladies to be mindful of the company you keep. I'm not just talking boys either. Some females can be very toxic to your growth as a maturing young woman," she told them as a few nodded.

"My crew is solid. Ain't no snakes in my circle," one girl said, tooting her lips out.

"Yeah. Until the circle breaks and she slithers away. Then what?"

The young girl, age fourteen, was stumped. She didn't have the answer to that. Right now, in her mind, she had the best crew of friends, and they may have been, but Harlem was just giving her a heads up. She experienced firsthand what it was like to have a snake bite her; repeatedly until she finally had to let it slither away. It was crazy how she was 'friends' with someone for years to only realize they were never really her friend.

"Well, until that time comes. I'm good."

"Okay, Princess. Just remember what I said. Now, on to resumes. Did you all print them out?" Harlem asked.

Everyone nodded and dug into their folders to retrieve their resumes they had been working on since group last week. Harlem had been working at the shelter going on five months, but she already had an amazing rapport with the women and their children. Groups were only on Wednesday's, and you better believe not one girl missed. They looked forward to meeting with Ms. Harlem. Not only did she motivate them to want to overcome their circumstances, but she could relate to them on more than just her doing her job. She wanted to help change their life even if it was just by the encouraging words she spoke.

Packing up her belongings for the day, Harlem grabbed her purse and locked up her office. Though she only worked five hours a day, Monday through Friday, they had given her an office space. It was nice and tidy; a place of peace where they could relax as she called it for her girls.

"Hey, boo. You gone for the day?" Kalli, a case manager, asked, strolling past Harlem's office.

"Yes. Gotta get home to my men," she chuckled.

"I know that's right with EJ's little handsome self. Well, I'll see you next week. Have a good weekend."

"You too," she said, waving bye.

Hopping in her car, the first thing she did was call Enzo. It was the first thing she did every day she got off work. With an inquisitive, walking eleven-month old in the crib, she just had to make sure her man was still alive.

"What up, baby. You off?" Enzo's voice boomed over her speaker. The speakers that belonged to a black G 500 Mercedes Benz truck. It was a 'just because he felt like buying it' gift from Enzo a few months ago. Since they planned to take their trip out of the country when Lil' Enzo turned one, Enzo had found other ways to make up for it until then. Small gifts here and there had become his specialty over time.

"Yes. Headed home now. What is my baby doing?"

"DaDaDaDa," Enzo junior blabbed loudly into the phone.

Harlem smiled at his baby talk but rolled her eyes too. "I think he does that on purpose. He should be saying mama knowing I'm the one who gave birth to him.

"Aww, don't be jealous, ma. Tell your mama don't be jealous," he chuckled, as little Enzo tugged at the bracelet on his wrist that said 'Enzo' in gold.

"Whatever. What you want to eat? I'll be home in like fifteen minutes."

"You," he said evenly, making Harlem squeeze her legs together tightly.

"Aight. I'ma hold you to that too. I had a long day."

Enzo licked his lips. "Good. I like when it been marinating and shit. It's well seasoned."

Harlem laughed out loud at his nasty mouth. "You are silly. I'll see y'all in a little bit."

"Aight. Drive safe."

When the call disconnected, Harlem still had a smile on her face. It was just something about getting off work from doing what she loved and coming home to her little family. She wouldn't trade it for anything in the world. When she pulled up to their house that Enzo promised her he would get, she pulled into the garage. Standing at the door anxious to see his woman, Enzo held his replica in his arms before letting him down. Little Enzo ran as fast as his tiny legs would allow him straight to Harlem.

"Hi, baby. Look at you," Harlem cooed, kissing all over his face and nestling her nose in the crook of his neck. "You just gave him a bath?"

"Yeah. He had shit all up his back after we ate some ice cream."

Harlem chuckled. "I told you he be cutting up. Hey, stinky," she grinned as he patted at her face.

"How was work?" Enzo questioned once they were inside.

"Interesting as always. You know every day is something different."

He nodded understanding completely. The opening of Heavy's Hookah Lounge was giving Enzo a run for his money. Business was good, but he'd be lying if he said it wasn't a stressful ass job. He was learning though, and with the help of Briscoe being the head cook, the two were looking to be open for a while.

"I hear that. I'm proud of you, though. You on your shit," Enzo praised, smacking her booty and delivering a kiss to her lips.

"Mmm. Thank you. You still want me for dinner? I think we can start early," she said, licking her lips and eyeing his dick print through his boxers.

Enzo was comfortable as ever while his son was dressed the same in a diaper. Grinning, he pulled her into him by the waist.

"Yeah. I got you," he said. His raspy voice sending chills down her spine.

"You promise?"

He nodded. "I got you always. Know that."

Smiling, Harlem pecked his lips again. "I got you too. For life."

Though she had been hesitant to let Enzo back in her life after his abrupt departure, Harlem was glad she didn't let her once cold heart stop her from doing so. When Enzo promised that he got her and wasn't leaving again, he meant that. There's a difference in a man saying he got you, and one showing he got you. The two are not the same and Enzo was a sole believer in letting his actions speak for him.

Their love had conquered all the hardships they faced together, and though they had taken many losses, lessons were learned along the way. The biggest ones learned was how to love and learn from their past mistakes. The love wasn't real if it didn't come with a struggle, right? Enzo and Harlem had struggled enough. The rest of their days were about to be celebrating their glow up and accomplishments.

There wasn't anything like coming from the bottom, sacrificing, starving, hungry for a better life, and finally making it out the hood. Yeah, it had raised Harlem, but it didn't stop her from becoming the woman she was today. If anything, it made her want to be greater. She was more than her chaotic life's circumstances, and if anyone didn't understand that, they didn't understand the real and what it meant to survive living in the Gutta.

The End

Keep reading for an exclusive sneak peek of my October release 'When She's Broken.'

ACKNOWLEDGMENTS

To my amazing readers, thank you so much! I pray you all enjoyed Harlem and Enzo's story as much as I did. The message behind it, is strong. Ladies, you are not your circumstances. You are more than the struggle life may have hit you with. More than the setbacks you've taken, the losses you've received, and heartbreaks you've endured. Take those losses and turn them into lessons and WIN! You are a winner, regardless of the outcome of your situation because you're still here to conquer another day. Give thanks and know that He only gives the hardest battles to the toughest soldiers.

If you loved this series, please drop me a *review*, tag me on social media, or inbox me. I'd love to hear your feedback. Do you think Lucci & Yaz deserve their own book? Let me know. As always, thank you for your continuous support. Keep reading for an exclusive sneak peek of my upcoming release, 'When She's Broken.'

WHEN SHE'S BROKEN

BriAnn Danae

WHEN SHE'S BROKEN

PROLOGUE

Lying stiff as a board, Astryd tried calming her rapid heartbeat down. Her nerves were damn near getting the best of her, but she couldn't allow them to. Not now. With her back facing him, her eyes were trained on the door leading to their bathroom. It was slightly cracked and letting in a glimmer of light. Inhaling a deep breath, she gently peeled the thick comforter from her frame and slowly eased from underneath the damp sheet. A thin layer of perspiration had long ago coated her body because she was so nervous. So anxious to finally be doing this.

Swallowing the anxiety down her throat, Astryd placed one foot onto the hardwood floor, and her body immediately froze with fear when she heard him begin to shift in bed. *Had I moved too much?* She thought as her closed eyes pooled with tears. He came in drunk five hours ago, a little past midnight, wanting sex. He always wanted sex even if she wasn't in the mood. A silent prayer was sent up to God. Astryd was begging him to let this "man" remain sleep. When a light snore escaped him and echoed through their bedroom, she sighed with relief before placing her other foot on the ground.

On shaky legs, she was finally on her feet. She gripped her cell tightly in her right hand, so it wouldn't slip out. The palms of her hands were extremely sweaty. Her stomach churned as realization settled in. Clad in all of her nakedness, Astryd carefully tiptoed to their bathroom being sure to avoid the spot on the wood floor that creaked loudly when stepped on. Sweat rolled down her back as she stepped inside. Too afraid to look back, not wanting to at this point, she rushed to their massive walk-in closet.

The bathroom echoed much too loudly for the phone call she was about to make. Leaving the closet door slightly ajar, Astryd scrambled on her knees to the furthest part of the closet, sat against the wall and pulled her knees to her chest. The plush carpet felt amazing against her naked frame, and honestly, if she could, she'd much rather sleep in the closet than lie in bed with him every night.

She stared at the entrance of the closet for over two minutes with her listening skills tuned in to any movement. When she didn't hear any was when she finally unlocked her phone. The brightness from the screen had been dimmed to the point you could hardly see a thing on it, but she had trained herself to see and read everything, even in darkness. She had been in it for so long; Astryd grew accustomed to it.

The ten-digit number she committed to memory stared back at her on the keypad. Having typed it more times than she'd like to admit; Astryd was finally ready to use it. Her hands shook uncontrollably, and chills covered her arms as the air conditioning kicked on.

I must do this.

In her mind, this was the only other option if she wanted her situation to change. Her life to change, yet again. All the bullshit, hurt, lies, pain, emotional and physical abuse he put her through had taken a toll on her. Not just her body, but her mind and soul as well. Her toxic relationship had drained her of the happiness she used to be filled with. The days of smiling because it was genuinely done were of the past.

Designer clothing draped over her head and shoulders as she tapped the green phone button to connect the call. The first ring rocked her core as she struggled to control her breathing. For months, she had been planning this, and now she didn't know if it were such a great idea. Before she could hang up and take what she assumed was the coward way out, the operator answered the phone.

"Hi, may I help you?"

Silence.

Astryd was stuck. She didn't know what words to even use after having rehearsed them in her head a thousand times.

"Hi. How can I help you?" the young woman spoke again.

"Hi," Astryd replied in her whisper soft tone.

"Hi, ma'am. How can I help you this morning?"

It was five in the morning. She was praying the young woman could help her. She needed anyone to help her at this point. Astryd couldn't help herself.

"Is this... is this the women's shelter?"

"It's the hotline for shelters, yes. Are you seeking shelter?"

Astryd's eyelids closed tightly. Her throat ached from the pain she felt having to answer the question, but she knew it had to be answered. Tears stung her eyes as she nodded her head.

"Yes. He's... he's so different now," she said more to herself.

"Are you currently in danger?" the woman asked as she began to take notes.

Astryd's eyes looked up to the door. When she didn't see him standing there, she shook her head from side to side.

"No. Not right now. I don't think I'm really in danger... I just. I guess I wanted to know my options," she let out quickly and quietly.

As the woman began to ask her an array of questions pertaining to her life, Astryd couldn't believe some of the things she had endured over the years. Her mind was boggled at the idea of being in a domestic violence relationship. To her, she just thought maybe he had gotten a little jealous over the years and loved her in a different way.

I'm being crazy. This was a bad idea.

"Hi. Are you still there?" the operator asked.

Astryd closed her eyes and sighed. "Yes. But, I think I'll just call back later. I don't think I can leave him yet."

"Are you sure? If you're in any danger, you can always call the poli-"

"Who you on the phone with?"

Astryd's eyes flew open, and she flinched so hard at the sound of his deep voice, the phone fell from her hand. When their eyes connected, she blinked back tears. Whatever answer he was looking for, she was terrified of giving it. In a pair of boxers and nothing else, he stood at the closet door with his hands behind his back waiting for her to answer him. Astryd shook her head from side to side.

"No one?" he questioned.

She shook her head again.

His jaw ticked. Making slow, long strides over to her, his 6'3 frame towered over hers as he bent down to pick up her phone. The operator was still on the line and she was silently praying for the timid young woman.

"Who the fuck is this?" he boomed, making Astryd scramble to scoot away from him. Grabbing her thigh, he squeezed it tightly, forcing her to stay directly in front of him.

The operator remained quiet. For confidentiality purposes, she couldn't disclose who she was or what she did.

Especially not in this type of situation. Astryd's life could be on the line. When she didn't answer, he chuckled.

"A'ight. You don't want to answer? Maybe she will," he grimaced, pulling a gun from behind him.

Astryd went to scream, but he stopped her.

"Nah. Don't make noise now. You trying to fucking leave me?" he hissed as the gun grazed Astryd's scalp.

Afraid to move her head, she spoke in a shaky breath terrified of the lie she was about to tell. "No."

"That's what I heard, though. You can't leave me now? Then, when? And, whoever this is was going to help you?" he gritted through clenched teeth, wanting to slap her across her beautiful face.

Again, she shook her head no as a tear rolled down her cheek.

"You love me?" he asked.

"Yes," she voiced.

"If you love me, why you trying to leave me then?"

"I'm not. I promise," she sniffled. "I love you."

"You hear that, mufucka? She loves me. But, clearly, she must love you too if she's trying to leave me. I hope you know you just got her killed."

BOOM!

Hopping up from her sleep, Astryd placed a hand on the side of her head and closed her eyes. *Fuck, it was a dream.* Her body was soaked in sweat and her heart was beating faster than it ever had in her life. Struggling to breathe, her body quaked as she began to cry. The warm body lying next to her lifted before pulling Astryd into its embrace.

"What's the matter?" he asked softly, wrapping his arms around her waist.

She shook her head trying to get back to reality. "It felt so real. This dream."

"But, it wasn't. It was probably just a nightmare," he reassured her, before kissing her cheek. "Let me get you something to drink."

Astryd nodded in the dark. "Okay."

When he climbed from the bed, she pulled her knees to her chest and sat staring at the bathroom door that was slightly opened displaying a glimmer of light. The same light in her dream. Her eyes were full of curiosity and hope. She was hoping this was the last dream she ever had like that. But, more importantly, she was curious as to why she was having it.

Should it have been me, first?

The question burned her up inside, and whatever answer she needed to ease her mind was never going to come. It was too late.

Coming in early October!

STAY CONNECTED

Join Going Beyond The Book Reading Group Facebook LIKE Page

OTHER BOOKS BY ME

Phresh & Nykee: Loving You Past The Pain 1-2

Juvie & Solai: A Hood Love Story

She Used To Be The Sweetest Girl (standalone)

He Want That Old Thang Back

In No Need For Love 1-2

My Heart Is A Fool Series

Feenin' For A G 1-2

Made in the USA
Las Vegas, NV
04 October 2024